Robin Hood to the Rescue!

WIDO . . . BEGAN HIS ENTERTAINMENT WITH A BALLAD

(See page 3)

Robin Hood to the Rescue!

By
AGNES BLUNDELL

Illustrated by Frank Rogers

ST. AIDAN PRESS, LLC
Morning View, Kentucky

Robin Hood to the Rescue!

First published in 1939 by Burns Oates & Washbourne Ltd., London.

Typesetting, layout and cover design copyright 2024 St. Aidan Press, LLC.

Cover art is a royalty-free image from *Medieval Design*, copyright 2007 by Dover Publications, Inc.

ISBN-13: 978-1-962503-12-9
ISBN-10: 1-962503-12-7

For more information, contact:
www.staidanpress.com
staidanpress@gmail.com

We have made no intentional change from the original text except to correct mistakes in spelling and punctuation.

Contents

Robin Hood to the Rescue!

CHAPTER ONE

IN THE MERRY days of old, there was no merrier place than Sherwood Forest, for though the jolly outlaw, Robin Hood, was a reformed character and had been rechristened and knighted by King Richard, he hunted the royal forests as blithely as ever. True, he no longer emptied travellers' pockets, nor made them pay toll, willy-nilly, when they crossed his domain, but he befriended the poor as stoutly as ever, and challenged any rich baron or tax-gatherer who dared to act unjustly.

Robin only used his title of Sir Adam de Everingham on state occasions, and though his headquarters were supposed to be in Barnsleydale where the King had granted him land, he was more often to be found in Sherwood, under a lodge of green boughs, or sleeping out on the open hill-side. His band of followers had followed his fortunes and had added the badges of Royal Rangers and Woodwards to their old uniforms of Lincoln Green. They were still the best bowmen in the countryside, and popular with all who had not evil deeds on their consciences.

The chief friends of Robin Hood and his lady, Maid Marian, were the noble Sir Aelfric de Southwell and his family. The Knight indeed was seldom at home, as he was one of Cœur de Lion's most trusted leaders, and was now busy in Normandy assisting his master to construct the new Castle Gaillard, or Saucy Castle, to overawe the French. His wife Etheldreda meanwhile

1

looked after the demesne, and her five children: Eadgar, who was page to the Bishop of Ely, Osmund, his junior by a year and now nearly thirteen, Hild, who would be twelve next birthday, Stephen, eight, and Sibell, four. They lived in a fortified Manor House next to Southwell Minster, and Eadgar was still at home because he was always given leave to return to Southwell for the great celebrations at Whitsuntide, the Minster having special privileges for this feast.

It was glorious June weather, and the Castle children were allowed to ramble at their will about the forest which covered the higher part of the country. The ground surrounding Southwell itself was extremely watery, for not only did the district boast at least seven wells, patronized since Roman times, but was traversed by the mighty River Trent and its tributary brooks. Etheldreda fondly imagined that she might at last enjoy a little peace, for her three great enemies, Guy de Gisburn, Hal of Nottingham, and Fulk de Brent, were now dead, and it seemed as though no one were likely to trouble her during her husband's absence, as had been the case on previous occasions. There had been many guests at the Manor during Whitsuntide, but all had now departed to their homes. Wido, the travelling minstrel, lingered behind and came up one evening to give a last entertainment before he took to the road again.

He was a great friend of the children, and his arrival was a delight to the whole Castle. Eadgar was never tired of listening to the immense romances which Wido could relate, partly in prose and partly in verse. Perhaps his favourite of all was the Romaunt of Arthur, a medley of thrilling tales, which Wido had picked up in Wales. Each separate story somehow hooked into three or four more, and there seemed no reason why the romaunt should ever come to an end.

Osmund loved the parts about jousts and fighting, but he thought the tales of magic very foolish.

"I'd much rather the knight just won by courage, Wido," he declared. "Magic is too easy—besides, it isn't real."

"I wouldn't be sure, young master," Wido always replied.

Soon everyone gathered in the Great Hall; the lady Etheldreda took her place near the hearth but with her chair turned round to face the room. Wido was tuning his lute as he paced about in front of her; the ladies of the household and the children sat in a semicircle on either side, while the maids, farmservants and men-at-arms assembled at the back. The Seneschal posted himself opposite the lady, as was his right, and the hinds and villeins crowded in at the far end of the hall.

Wido had a fine baritone voice, and began his entertainment with a ballad. Everyone clasped hands and swung arms and body in time to the tune, rather in the way people do when they sing Auld Lang Syne nowadays. It was a new ballad all about a knight who parted from the lady he loved to go to the Holy Wars, and of how he came back long years afterwards disguised as a pilgrim to find out if his lady had kept faith with him. He met a false friend, who declared that his Adeliza had forgotten him and married the Lord of Castles Three, so the pilgrim rushed into the forest wide and became a hermit. After that the children rather lost the thread of the tale, but it ended tragically as such ballads always did. The lady dismissed the wicked lord and began to pine away, and somehow or other she wandered into the forest glade and died of grief just outside the hermitage while the hermit was at his orisons within.

"It's not a bit like what would really happen," muttered Eadgar. "Hermits retire from the world to think about God—not about faithless ladies."

"He ought to have slain the Lord of Castles Three," declared Osmund, "didn't he, Wido? Didn't he slay the false knight?"

"The ballad does not say so," replied Wido, twanging his lute crossly. He disliked any interruption and could not bear to be criticized. "Maybe the spectre cold of the hermit bold that night to him appeared——"

This time it was Stephen who interrupted. "I don't like it," he cried loudly.

The lady Etheldreda shook her head at the gleeman. She had warned him beforehand not to mention either spectres or witches as she did not want Stephen and Sibell to be frightened.

A minstrel had to please the lady of the Manor at all costs, so he smiled, asked a riddle which had a punning answer and began another tale.

"Once upon a time," he said, "there was a hill shepherd in Wales. He was so poor that he had nothing at all of his own. One day his master called him and bid him drive his flock to London town and sell it there as the price of wool in Wales had fallen. So the shepherd cut a stout hazel staff from the thicket and went his way. 'Twas a long journey, but he beguiled the time by singing the old ballads with which the Welsh entertain each other when they meet in the warm farmhouses and make merry, when the snow is on the hill." Here Wido burst into song:

> "King Arthur of the Table Round
> A mighty man was he
> With his Knights so bold
> And his crown of gold
> And his Kingdom from sea to sea."

"It wasn't really from sea to sea," began Eadgar, but everyone else said:

"Hush!"

"Well, you know all about King Arthur, it seems," cried Wido quickly dropping into prose again. "Suffice it then to say that under his rule the Cymri were a great and valiant nation. When Arthur fell in battle, he was mourned by mortals and all in the land of faerie, but a rumour grew that Arthur was not dead, but would return when the times were ripe and rule over his land again in peace and glory. 'Twas the prophecy, too, of Merlin the magician, who wrote hundreds of prophecies in mystic verses called triads, which the Welsh preserve with great reverence."

"Have any of them come true?" inquired Eadgar.

"Of course, or they wouldn't have been prophecies," retorted Wido, and passed rapidly on, lest the young scholar should be inclined to argue the point.

> "The shepherd left his mountains
> In the land of singing streams,
> In the land of night-born fountains,
> In the land of radiant gleams;
> And he came to London town,
> And on London bridge stood he,
> And he gazed up-river and down
> In bewildered reverie—

"That is to say, he was so astounded, poor, simple fellow, at the array of shops and booths on each side of the bridge, and at all the boats of merchandise and the wherries plying for hire down below, and at the bawling of the merchants' varlets, proclaiming their wares, and all the bustle of town, that he was as one stunned. More than one rogue slipped a hand in his pocket, but 'twas empty. He had sold the sheep, lodged the money with a merchant, as his master had bid him, and slipped the luck-penny into his shoe. Presently as he stood still, craning his neck over the parapet, a hand fell on his shoulder, and a voice asked him a question. The shepherd whirled round and saw a stranger in a big cloak with a large book under his arm. 'I have no English,' he said, very respectfully, for he saw at once that his questioner was a wise man.

"'Where got you yon speckled staff?' said he, in very good North-country Welsh.

"'In my own land,' said the shepherd.

5

"'Take me to the place and your fortune is made,' said the wise man. 'For I can tell by the look of your staff, that under the roots of that hazel lies buried a vast treasure of gold and silver.'"

At this point the lady turned the hour sand-glass, which stood on a stool beside her. Wido took the hint and condensed his story.

"In a week and a day, the two men were standing on the sheep-walk at the very spot," he went on. "The stranger said some queer words out of his book, and moved a stone at the root of the hazel. A big hole opened out before them and steps leading down into a vast cavern. 'Follow me,' said the magician. 'But mind how you go. We shall pass three great bells and if you touch any of them, we are both dead men.' So saying, he stepped briskly down the stairs and the shepherd followed him into a huge subterranean chamber. In the centre was a circular table round which lay knights in armour with their weapons beside them. The shepherd marked one taller than the rest, with a crown of gold on his head and a red dragon on his shield. The table was piled with gold and silver dishes, bags of coin and bowls of precious stones. 'Take what you like but make no noise,' said the wise man.

"Now the shepherd had never seen such riches in his life, and he seized the biggest and heaviest he could and hurried to the stairs, meaning to put his treasure in a safe place and come back for more. He was in such haste that he forgot to be careful, and a long bar of gold struck against one of the bells as he staggered by. Oh! what a noise it made, like all the thunderstorms you have heard, rolled into one. The shepherd nearly died of fright! The warriors in the cave leaped up from sleep and seized their arms, but when the wise man shouted above the tumult: 'The time is not yet!' they all sank down again, and the shepherd and the magician dropped their treasure and fled into the open air. 'You fool,' said the magician, 'you did not heed my warning, and now you have broken the spell. Whoever looks upon Arthur again until his hour comes, is doomed to wither away and die.'

"With that, he pushed back the stone and stamped it down. The shepherd ran home, meaning to come back some other day, but search as he might, he never found the place again and never again set eyes on the wise man. The few jewels which he had slipped into his pocket, made him rich enough to buy a farm on which he lived happily ever after."

As soon as Wido finished the lady Etheldreda made a sign to the Seneschal who made a sign to the steward who made a sign to the pantrymen. Everyone got up, the shepherd, the swineherd, and the hayward withdrew into a group, as behoved freemen, while the grooms and villeins lifted out the trestle tables which had been laid against the wall, and the cook and his underlings hurried away to send in supper.

Hild remained dreamily sitting in the rushes, and Alice had to call her three times before she could get her attention.

The elder children were expected to help in the serving and then to take their places next their mother at the high table, where the lady kept a watchful eye on all that was going on, and noted any waste or slovenliness with a prompt reproof. Stephen and Sibell were carried off to bed where they were regaled with honey possets as a treat. Wido tucked into boar's ham with a good appetite, and Hild set a dish of dried plums near him, for she knew his fondness for this form of dessert. Dried fruit and sugar plums were only served on special occasions.

CHAPTER TWO

SOUTHWELL VILLAGE was built on low-lying land, but on the north and west rose a series of wooded hills interspersed with marshy valleys, known locally as 'dumbles.' Besides discovering the springs of salubrious water, the Romans had built roads and villas in the neighbourhood; the remains of one of these houses, sunk deep in a cleft in the woodland, was the children's favourite place, and this summer they were determined to trace out the course of the paved road which had once run past it, but which had long since been lost and forgotten.

Eadgar was a dreamy, studious boy, who could be happy for hours writing a chronicle in a sheepskin book which Osmund and Hild had made for him as a Christmas present. Even when he was not illuminating initial letters, or poring over the carefully written page, he was thinking about it and composing the bit he would write next in the stiffest and most solemn style he could invent. The chronicle was written in English, at Hild's request, and Eadgar was rather ashamed of a composition in the vernacular, and felt bound to make it as dignified as he could to atone for not writing in Latin or even French. The discovery of the remains of the Roman villa and their adventures of the previous year made an interesting chapter, for Eadgar's work was exclusively concerned with the happenings of his own time.

"We must find out exactly where the old road goes," he remarked one day. "I could make a map of it, if we once traced it out."

"It can't go very far," said Osmund, "we have ridden or walked all through the country and there is no road which corresponds to this one."

"We know the southern end goes through the marsh and joins the lane," pursued Eadgar. "But we don't know exactly about the other direction—it was lost under the brambles."

Eadgar sat down on a fallen tree staring unseeingly at the fluttering leaves, among which warblers and titmice were busily seeking provender for the young birds whose lisping notes sounded loudly from hidden nests. Presently Hild approached, and planted herself before him.

"Eadgar, do let us do something interesting," she pleaded. "Osmund and Stephen are practising with their bows, and I've scraped my finger—look!—and it is too sore to shoot any more."

"You should use your glove," said Eadgar. "You might skin your wrist badly."

"I know, but I didn't," retorted Hild. "It is nothing much and I have washed it in the brook. Do come for a walk," she added coaxingly. "Perhaps if you and I went softly together, without any loud talking, we might discover the way the road goes when it leaves the cleft."

"You speak as if the road made a noise like a stream," said her brother, laughing. "Come on then, let us go and listen for the road."

Having gained her point Hild did not mind a little teasing.

Curiously enough the villa was hidden in a deep valley—the Romans had evidently made use of an existing road, and built their dwelling beside it. It lay some twenty feet below the level of the surrounding land.

Hild led the way up the bank at a brisk pace and, forgetting all about the wise and solemn exploring she had suggested, she began to run along the edge of the ravine, laughing, singing and talking, sometimes dodging into the wood or pausing in a clearing to pluck wild roses.

Eadgar followed and soon the walk became a race. Hild tucked her long plaits into her tunic that they might not catch in the branches, and bounded ahead, pushing her way through bushes and briars with an impatience which recked nothing of the damage done to clothes and stocking, until at length they came out of the wood into an open space of unfenced pasture.

Isolated groups of nut bushes were dotted about near the edge of the wood: they looked like islands in the rippling sea of flowery grass. As Eadgar gazed he became aware of a strip of turf, darker green than the rest and raised a foot or two above the meadow surface. It stretched away before them, five yards broad, almost from their very feet to the top of the grassy hill which bounded the horizon.

"It's as straight as if it had been drawn with a ruler," said the boy in an awed voice.

"What?" asked Hild. "Where?" she added wonderingly.

"Don't you see?" he answered. "The road—the Roman road."

"Does it go all the way to Rome, do you suppose?" inquired Hild, wading through the grass towards it.

"Well, it couldn't go across the sea, of course, and we have our backs to Rome now—we are looking north," said Eadgar dreamily.

Hild whirled round as though she expected to see the pinnacles of the Eternal City behind her; but there was only the wood, with the deepening glow of June sunlight gilding the top-most boughs.

"This old track must be our road," she whispered. "Do let us see where it goes to! Come quick—let's run along the Roman road!"

Her excitement infected Eadgar. He could not tell how it was that the road should show so plainly now as though it had risen up through the bosom of the meadow. Hild clutched his hand and together they went solemnly forward through the tall buttercups until their feet left the spongy ground and struck upon a hardness which told of buried pavements. Then they began to run, enchanted by the discovery and the magic of the hour. The secret, buried road had risen into the open and lured them on. Half-laughing, half-awed they sped up it together, slowing down sometimes for a few paces to get their breath, and then flying onward once more.

Eadgar had only meant to go a little way, but, once started, an irresistible fascination drew him on. If only they could get to the top of the hill and find out if the Road was still discernible on the further slope! Hild had at first been as eager as he, but at length her steps began to flag, and she stopped with a little cry of dismay.

"It's getting dark!"

Eadgar felt as though wakened with a jolt from a delicious dream. The sun had sunk behind the tall trees and, when they turned and stared backwards, the straight ribbon of the road had vanished. It was some special effect of the evening rays which had made its course appear so plain; now that they were withdrawn the whole surface of the grassy plain seemed even.

"It's gone!" faltered Hild in terror.

"No, it hasn't. You can feel it underfoot." Eadgar stamped on the sod. "Come, we must go back quickly. There's no reason to be afraid—we can see the wood from here—and anyhow the country is quiet enough."

"I'm not afraid," declared the girl, but her pale face belied the words. "'Tis passing strange though—almost as though we had been bewitched. Let's run!"

They started off at a brisk pace but in a few minutes Hild was floundering in a marsh.

"I've stepped off the path somehow," she called in alarm.

11

As Eadgar came to help she noted that his stockings, too, were wet and muddy.

"We must go back to where we were standing," he said cheerfully, "just over there—see where our feet have crushed down the grass."

They tried to retrace their steps, both concealing their anxiety.

"We didn't come through this patch of sedges," declared Hild. "Try and think where the nearest road is, Eadgar. You have ridden over all this country with Osmund."

"Yes, we'll find a road, of course," answered Eadgar. "But I haven't been much at home these last three years. If we find our own Roman road again it will take us straight back."

"You said we were facing north when we started," said his sister. "But if we had been wouldn't the setting sun have been on our left—'twas behind us surely?"

They debated this point for some minutes, their feet sinking meanwhile in the spongy soil.

"I think we had better go on to the top of the hill," Eadgar decided at last. "We are sure to see some house from there—perhaps we shall be able to see the Manor—or we'll find a shepherd or someone who can guide us."

"I'm afraid of falling into a bog," said Hild.

"Take my hand, I'll go first," answered Eadgar.

He went forward uphill, and the girl pattered after him. It no longer seemed a glorious and dazzling adventure, and Hild kept thinking of the lady Etheldreda and of what her feelings would be when the other two boys came home alone.

"Now you really are a distressed maiden," cried Eadgar, laughing to cheer her. "And I'm a Knight Errant—rather more errant than I could wish at this moment; but we're really not far from home."

"I smell wood-smoke," whispered Hild. "What if it should be——"

"Why, it might be our good friend, Robin Hood!" cried Eadgar joyfully. He sprang ahead and was pushing eagerly through the low bushes of dwarf willow and hazel which covered the hill top, when he was sharply challenged, and heard the warning click of a cross-bow.

"Hold, friend!" cried the boy. "I bear no arms, and only seek to be directed to Southwell."

Instead of the friendly group of jolly foresters, shepherds or charcoal-burners whom he expected to see, a grim little band of men rose up silently out of the grass.

Eadgar recoiled, thrusting Hild behind him, but it was too late. There was a muttered order, and the children were roughly seized.

A fire was smouldering in the centre of a ring of trampled grass, but there was no roasting venison such as Robin Hood would have provided. The figures that surrounded them looked more like those of sea-faring men: they had red, weather-beaten faces and gold rings in their ears, and wore heavy woollen tunics. They spoke with a South-country accent, strange to Eadgar's ears.

"They two will be better nor nothing," said one fellow. "They be gentle nurtured, I do allow, and that do always fetch its price."

"We come from Southwell Castle," said Hild eagerly. "The lady will give you a good reward if you take us home in safety."

"Yes, sure," answered the fellow. "A crown piece and a drink o' sour ale and all the monks' minions will be set on our heels after. What will this one fetch, think 'ee?" he asked, and catching Eadgar suddenly by the back of the neck, he flung him sprawling on the grass before his fellows. They all laughed brutally, and the boy sprang up, scarlet with anger.

"Beware how you touch me, churls that you are! I have been the King's page and now serve the Lord Bishop of Ely!" he cried.

"He be worth a fair pound o' weighed silver in Ireland," declared the leader of the band. "But the wench is over young though she is fair-favoured."

He was about to catch Hild by the hair in order to drag her forward into the firelight, but Eadgar rushed between and pushed away the villain's hand. He was instantly felled to the ground again, and Hild shrieked for help with all her might. Her voice had no more effect than the cry of a frightened bird, and the ugly threats with which she was assailed quickly reduced her to silence. The young prisoners were now bound and gagged and forced to sit down on the grass while their captors decided on their fate. The children gathered from what they heard that the men were a band of slavers from Bristol where the horrid trade was still carried on in secret in spite of the vigorous disapproval of the Church. Chieftains in the wilder parts of Ireland were always ready to purchase slaves, especially those who had been gently reared, but the chief of the slavers, whose name was Eli, was of opinion that it would not be possible to get so far across country with their prey.

"It will be safer to get rid of them in Wales," he declared. "E'en if we have to return to the ship empty-handed. Saddle the beasts, boys—we must start at once."

On this point they were all agreed. It would not do to linger in the neighbourhood. While they argued together Eadgar managed to pull off his woollen garter and tie it round a hazel twig. Presently a string of horses were led out of the bushes and saddled, bundles were re-distributed and Eadgar and Hild were each mounted in front of one of the seamen.

The horses were good and had been well rested. The men seemed to know the country and set off at a round pace. They crossed the rivers at lonely fords and avoided every village and group of houses clustered round a Manor or Abbey.

Eadgar prayed desperately that they might be waylaid and questioned or overtaken by his mother's men-at-arms. He reproached himself bitterly for his folly, though he could not have foreseen the danger into which they had fallen headlong. No one had ever heard of slavers in their quiet, settled part of the country, though there were horrid rumours of their raids in Northumberland and on the turbulent border. It was said the chieftains there sold the prisoners they had captured in their forays, though it was against the law and severely punished by the lord Marchers if the guilt could be brought home.

But no one met or stayed them. The scouts who rode ahead were much too clever, and though the captives saw twinkling lights afar off in comfortable houses, they could do nothing to make their plight known and felt themselves carried every hour further and further from home and safety.

CHAPTER THREE

THE FITZ-AELFRICS were a very united family and liked doing things together, and Osmund was annoyed when he discovered that Eadgar and Hild had disappeared.

"The other two have gone off exploring without us," he grumbled to Stephen. "I don't think it's fair."

Stephen was angry too.

"That's too bad!" he cried. "Why didn't you stop them? And now we'll have to go home because I've got my sleeves wet in the brook."

Stephen came slowly stumping up to his brother: he was rather tired with his exertions and not averse to going home a little earlier than usual, but he would have died rather than admit it.

"Oh, bother!" cried Osmund, and he threw down the chisel, with which he had been shaping tesseræ, with such violence that several of the neat little red sandstone squares were broken.

"I wanted to explore the road! Why couldn't we have gone too?" protested Stephen.

"They can't have got very far as they haven't taken the bill-hook," cried Osmund. "The brambles are much thicker and stronger now than they were when we scrambled through in the spring, and it only leads to an old land-slide, anyhow. Let's run home—if the others don't find us here it's their own fault."

"I suppose they will go straight to the Manor if they are late," answered Stephen. "We can give a call or two presently."

16

They scrambled into the wood, and Osmund blew the little hunting-horn he carried slung on his belt. Then they both gave their own particular family rallying cry: "Whoo-whoo-ee!" but there was no answer.

When they reached the Manor there was no sign of the others, and Dame Alice, the old nurse, was very angry about Stephen's wet sleeves. When she discovered that Eadgar and Hild were missing, she informed the lady at once, following up with the story of Stephen's plight and ending with the demand that all playing in the wood should be forbidden. Then she drew a long breath and began all over again, but the lady did not seem to be listening very attentively. She chid herself for being over-fearful, but all the same her face grew pale and she stepped hurriedly to the window and pushed back the shutter.

"They will return before long," Osmund assured her. "No doubt Eadgar has lost his way—and Hild does not know the wood as well as I do."

Etheldreda leaned out, looking anxiously towards the dark trees.

"Nothing could happen to them," repeated Osmund.

"Son, go and call my lieutenant," said the lady. "Why do you hesitate? Do my bidding this instant!"

"I was only thinking that all the men are up on the pastures at the shearing," said the boy. "But I'll call Master Algar—and, mother—may I ride with him?"

"It's my belief nothing but trouble comes of this wandering outside the garden," broke in Dame Alice. "Dirty chausses, children staying out late, and now my poor little lad with his arms soaked——"

"Go, dame, go hence—put Stephen to bed. Nay, wait—Stephen, I must know when and where you saw Hild last? Had you quarrelled that you were not all together?"

Osmund had departed on his message, and Stephen was alone with his mother.

"We hadn't quarrelled at all," he declared. "I should have been angry though, if I had known they were going without us," he added honestly.

"Eadgar should know better than to stay out after sunset," said the lady, moving restlessly to the window again.

Stephen did not feel at all alarmed, but he knew that both Eadgar and Hild would be penanced for their heedlessness. They would probably be forbidden to go outside the garth for two or three days, and of course this would stop all the fun in the wood. He stood quite still listening to the distant tramp of the lieutenant's heavy jack-boots as he slowly mounted the stone stairs. Osmund's flying footsteps were soon heard and he came panting in, made the scantiest bow as he held up the door-curtain and then rushed up to his mother.

"Lady, Mott the forester is below, saddling his horse. May I go too and show him which way they went on leaving us? We'll soon find them, never fear!"

Etheldreda gave her consent and Osmund dashed away again. Stephen was ordered to bed to his great disappointment; he went slowly up the spiral stairs which led to the children's room, and on the way peeped into the lady's bower where Hild slept on a little pallet bed at the foot of the lady's big one. The floor of the bower was strewn with scented rushes and Stephen paused in the doorway to sniff appreciatively.

Osmund thought it fine fun to go out riding after sunset, and he hurried with the forester to a clearing not far from the secret road. Here they tied their horses to trees and Osmund guided Mott to the place where trampled grass and bramble showed that the children had passed. It was still light enough for the quick-eyed woodman to descry sundry threads of wool

18

clinging to the briars, which Osmund identified as belonging to Eadgar's clothing. It was quite easy to follow their track and Mott shook his head over the bad woodcraft and was inclined to chide Osmund for his desire to hurry.

"Nay, nay, we'll not go back for the beasts," he declared. "Fair and softly, fair and softly, young master! No tracker will gallop over the slot of the deer."

The boy left him before the phrase was finished and ran and walked by turns until he broke through the bushes at the edge of the wood and came panting to the open pasture. There he shouted and shouted again, but there was no reply, only a startled owl flew out of a fir tree and sailed away over the grassy plain as silently as though his wings had been clothed with wool instead of feathers. Osmund soon found tracks through the grass, and he went forward, heedless of danger, at a rapid pace.

The wind had died down, and the tinkling of a stream could be heard in the stillness. Overhead the sky was serene and blue, with green bars on the western horizon. Every now and then the fragrance of meadow-sweet was wafted to Osmund's nostrils. He followed a false trail where Hild had blundered off the road and came back again, and presently summoned Mott with a shrill halloo.

The woodman found the boy standing in the coppice where the ashes of a recent fire were still smouldering.

"They had horses," he said breathlessly. "Quick—Mott—say how many horses there may have been here?"

"Not so fast, young master!" began the man as usual. "Why, who is to say yet that is aught but a tinkers' camp? *Pardi*, 'tis like enough our Eadgar is at home by now——"

"Nay, look!"

Osmund held up his brother's woollen garter, which he had found tied round a hazel twig.

THERE HE SHOUTED . . . BUT THERE WAS NO REPLY; ONLY A STARTLED
OWL FLEW OUT

(*See page* 19)

"He left that as a sign. It must mean they are in danger and we must act at once. Do thou follow the trail and I will go and call out our men. How old is the trail, Mott, say? Listen, maybe they are near still."

They sank down behind a bush, holding their breath. Osmund could hear nothing but the loud beating of his own heart. After a moment or two Mott began to move about on his hands and knees. After a careful examination of the charred wood he opined that the brands had been quenched two hours agone. While he was still deliberating as to whether it was right for him to let Osmund return alone, the boy left him and pushed his way through the bushes.

It is difficult to hurry when one is breathless and in great anxiety and when one's tired legs begin to feel like bars of lead. The ground was soft too—water welled up round Osmund's feet at each step, but presently something wonderful happened. As he was staring ahead, trying to gauge the distance to the dark border of the wood, he perceived a path outlined before him, straight as an arrow, darker in shade than the surrounding grass. He made towards it, scrambled up the steep side and went forward, marvelling, along the secret road that seemed to have risen out of the meadow at his need.

When the wood was reached, Osmund kept along the outer edge until he reached the ox-drove. He was about to leap the low hedge, when the sound of angry voices and the noise of stout blows made him pause. On the other side of the fence two men were struggling fiercely. The quarter-staffs with which they had at first been fighting had been flung aside and they were now using their fists. Though one man was decidedly larger and heavier than the other, the battle seemed to be equal and terrific blows were exchanged without either champion showing any signs of yielding. One was clad in archer's green, the other in tattered rags, and his beggar's bundles were lying at the wayside.

Osmund was about to continue his way—prudently keeping the hedge between himself and the disputants—when the larger of the two suddenly shouted for mercy.

"Hold thy hand—I yield!" he cried.

The other instantly stepped back, dropping his hands. His foe, who had feigned to sink to the ground, sprang up with a huge stone in his hands which he dashed down on his opponent's head.

"Shame!" shouted Osmund.

"A Robin!" roared the archer, as he reeled back.

The boy jumped over the hedge, ripping his tunic on the way. There was no time to pick and choose prudently, and though there were many Robins in the world besides Robin Hood, there was a likelihood that the reformed outlaw might be at his tricks once more.

The huge beggar picked up his stone again, and was lifting it high with the intention of crushing his adversary's skull, when Osmund put down his head and ran at him. It was not a knightly mode of attack, but it was successful. Boy and beggar fell together and rolled in the dust, and as he struggled to free himself Osmund heard the well-known, sweet bugle-notes ringing gaily through the evening air.

Tantivy—tantivy—tan-tallo!

The beggar had dropped the stone in his fall, and now began thumping Osmund with all his strength, but a strong hand soon plucked the boy out of his grasp, and Osmund found himself panting for breath, with Robin Hood on one side and his huge henchman, Little-John, on the other. Yes, it was Robin Hood sure enough, though he was disguised as a common archer and his brow was dripping with blood.

"Thou'rt well a-paid, Robin!" cried Little-John indignantly. "Why must thou ever go brawling without friends at thy back? But I'll pay this rogue his score—full measure, too!"

Little-John brandished a fist nearly the size of a leg of mutton in the astonished beggar's face, and then whipping a huge cudgel from his belt, he prepared to administer a terrific beating. Robin Hood interfered.

"Nay, nay! Little-John! The man is a stout, hardy fellow and will make a good henchman when he has learnt fair play——"

Osmund interrupted:

"Robin, you came in the nick of time. Eadgar and Hild have been carried away and we never needed your help more sorely."

The forester shot a keen glance at him. He knew Osmund of old and judged that this was no childish false alarm. He held up his hand to still the clamour of his comrades who had gathered round, furiously demanding leave to punish the beggar for his insolence. Then he questioned Osmund in quick, sharp, phrases.

"Have you searched the woods? Our Eadgar hath no great sense of direction."

"Yes, we have searched and called. But, Robin—Mott, our woodman, and I traced them to a thicket yonder, and the ground is all trampled by horses, and we found the embers of a fire, which have been quenched these two hours, Mott says."

"Has there been any talk of slavers being seen hereabouts?" asked Robin—he was still Robin Hood to all his friends and only used his title 'Sir Adam of Everingham' on state occasions.

"Slavers!" repeated Osmund in amazement.

"Aye, those sea-faring villains from Bristol have been abroad again. We have traced them down from Barnsleydale, but they gave us the slip in the Peak country. Hark ye, friend," he added, turning to his late antagonist. "Canst tell us aught of this?"

The beggar was crouching over his bundles, and now raised a bruised and surly face.

"An I could I wouldn't," he declared vengefully; then, as he caught Little-John's angry eyes, he added hastily: "I'm an honest beggar and would scorn to hold any traffic with such base folk."

"Nevertheless, you might have heard news among the travelling community," said Robin. "And you'll be no loser if you help us. There'll be a hue and cry raised for this lad, for he is the son of a noble knight and the King's page withal!"

"Thou hast broken my head," growled the beggar, "but I have broken thine also, and bear no malice," he added, cheering up. "I did meet a party of queer folk this very noon, watering their horses at the old ford up yonder—but they had no prisoners with them or young folk of any kind."

"That news hath called out the first and last angel thou'rt ever likely to meet!" cried Robin, tossing a gold coin to him as he spoke. "How many men? Good horses?"

"A dozen or fifteen—I did not count, and all on good beasts," replied the beggar, a beaming smile lighting up his face as he caught the gold piece and tested it in his strong teeth before thrusting it into his stocking.

"We've two horses tied in the wood," said Osmund eagerly. "And I was running home to send word to our men, who are all up on the pastures, while Mott tries to make out the trail."

"Our cattle are tired," returned the forester. "Go you, Tuck, to the lady and tell her Osmund is with me. Bid her send her men down the western road towards Cannock Chase, and call out the Verderer and his folk. Beggar, we shall meet again—thou didst deal me a foul blow and I'll be venged of it in fair fight. John, I leave you in charge of the band—get fresh horses and follow me."

"Where?" demanded the giant, planting himself in his chief's path with his huge arms akimbo.

"Why, thou must follow my track! Blackbird, lead on to thy horses. Fear not, we'll overtake them—if not tonight, by dawn."

Osmund was glad when his friend called him by his old nickname, bestowed upon him in jest, and going by contrary like all the nicknames of Robin's band. He glanced up at his friend anxiously as they hurried along, but could make nothing of the forester's expression. It was impossible to ask questions— all he could do was to answer Robin's queries as they ran.

"Thou'rt leading me astray, Blackbird—the horses are to the left of us," interrupted Robin suddenly.

He strode ahead, and led the way unerringly to the spot where the tethered beasts were stamping and fretting at the flies. Robin vaulted into the saddle without touching it with his hand, and stooped his green-hooded head as he guided his steed rapidly between the close-growing trees. Soon they were galloping single-file across the pasture-land, startling the water-birds, which rose up with a clatter of wings from the pools where they were feeding. Mott was overtaken about half a mile from the slavers' camp. The track of hoof-marks on the turf was fresh enough and could be seen even in the dim light. Robin sat still for a good five minutes, silently reflecting. Then he smote his knee angrily with his hand.

"They turned due west, mark ye, master, at this cross-roads," announced Mott. "They had some bit of a parley, I reckon, by the way the marks are set—the horses must have been reined up and fidgeting, as I make out, for I——"

"Blackbird—it will be a long night-ride, and maybe a skirmish at the finish. I'll leave thee here with Mott."

"Nay, Master Robin, nay! This is my quest! Let me come with you," begged Osmund.

"Follow, then," said the forester, and his heel touched the horse, which instantly moved off at a sharp trot.

Mott had not time to finish drawing the long breath he had begun to inhale preparatory to giving an immense exposition of his deductions from the marks in the grass, when he found himself alone again with only the gentle night-sounds for company. Robin was galloping his horse now, though the track was ill-paved and dangerous—yes, Mott decided, they had left the grass lane for a paved road.

25

"Where do you think they have gone, Master Robin?" asked Osmund, as they walked their horses down a stony incline.

"To the Welsh border," returned Robin briefly. "Eighty miles if 'tis an inch."

Osmund found it all he could do to keep up, and later in the night all he could do to stick in the saddle, leaving his horse to follow Robin's as best it could.

But fast as they rode, the slavers went faster yet. Robin paused sometimes at little taverns and lonely homesteads, and learned that mounted men had passed, clad like seafarers and armed like bandits. Sometimes they seemed hard on their heels, sometimes to have lost their traces altogether, and when dawn came they found themselves on a wide, trackless moor, out of sight of all human habitation.

CHAPTER FOUR

THE FUTURE LOOKED black enough as Robin Hood and Osmund led their horses across the waste, going afoot to ease their cramped limbs and to save the tired beasts.

"Master Robin, have you any friends in Wales?" queried the boy.

"Nay, and I know nought about the Welsh save a rude rhyme," returned the forester, and he began to sing:

> "Taffy was a Welshman,
> Taffy was a thief,
> Taffy came to my house
> And stole a leg of beef!"

"That would cost thee thy life were it the other side of the marches," cried a strange voice.

Osmund gazed about but could see no one. Robin leaped to the ground and had his bow in hand at the first word: he kept his fingers on the quiver, though he did not draw forth a bolt—he laughed.

"You are right, friend," he answered. "But in truth I would not be so uncourteous. I pray your pardon if you belong to that valiant nation."

"Who spoke and where is he?" asked Osmund. He could not help thinking of Wido's accounts of magic—invisible knights bent on evil abounded in the minstrel's tales.

"Yonder, in the thick reeds," said Robin in a low voice.

They were near a marshy stream, and some tall sedges were

growing in the water. The rustling, grey-green leaves seemed too sparse to hide a man, yet when Osmund followed the direction of Robin's eyes he saw something stirring among them, and presently a small, dwarfish creature came creeping out and advanced towards them.

He saluted with both hands flung high in the air, to show that he intended no attack.

Osmund rubbed his eyes and stared and stared again, for the Welshman—if such he was—seemed to belong to a fairy-tale rather than real life. He was under five foot in height and somewhat misshapen. His beard and hair were matted and his eyes glared feverishly. He wore a tarnished shirt of chain mail over leather breeches, and his bow-legs were defended by 'rusty banded chausses,' or hosen as the Saxons called them. But if his armour was neglected his arms were bright enough: a sword trailed in the wet grass, and two bright, naked daggers were thrust through his belt.

"Well met," said Robin. "Can'st thou tell us, honest comrade, where we may break our fast? We have ridden far, and my young friend here is sore weary."

The stranger fixed his dark-blue eyes on Osmund and addressed him without noticing Robin's query.

"Why dost thou seek friends in Wales, young Saxon?"

Osmund glanced at Robin for leave to answer, and his friend nodded.

"We're on the track of a party of false slavers who have carried off my brother and sister," he said.

"You are twenty miles from the border," said the dwarf. "But perhaps we can help each other. I have bread in my wallet, and I was cleaning the fish I have taken in the brook when I heard your voices. Will you eat with me? We can kindle a fire without much fear, for there is not likely to be anyone astir for another two hours."

"We must take heed where we light fire, though," said Robin. "For the earth of these turbaries, once set a-glow, will burn for six months at a stretch."

"I've no friends hereabouts, and care not if the whole kingdom burns," said the stranger vengefully. "I did but cross the dyke in arms to pursue my private enemy, and the whole country came out like a swarm of bees."

As he went grumbling back to the stream, Robin murmured to Osmund:

"He speaks of the great earthwork which King Offa built of old to hem in the Welshmen. They say it ran from sea to sea, or at any rate from the Dee to the Wye. And my rhyme is true enough, for it means the Welsh are constantly bursting out and seizing their neighbours' cattle."

"Is he a border cattle-thief, then?" asked the boy.

"Beshrew me, no! I take it he is a free-lance of sorts," said Robin, "and any Welshman found in arms on this side of Offa's Dyke is condemned to death without trial by Harold's ancient law."

"Then if we help him to get back in our company——"

Robin silenced him by a touch: the little Welshman was coming towards them with two or three small fish dangling from his hand.

"Eat, and then try and sleep," went on the forester as he took out the horses' bits, slackened the girths without removing the saddles—for the beasts were warm—and tethered each to a tough ground-willow bush. "We must go softly here and trust to gather knowledge which will save time later. Trust me, Osmund."

"Indeed I do, Robin," cried the boy.

"I would Little-John and our knaves would come up, for I am lightly provisioned both for arms and money," continued Robin. "Nevertheless, I'll stake a hundred crowns to one that within three days we'll have our birds safe out of the fowler's snare."

Three days seemed a long time to Osmund.

"Hild will be frightened," he said in a low voice. "And our mother will be wild with anxiety. Could we not call out the nearest Lord Marcher, Robin? You are Sir Adam de Everingham now and a Royal Forester to boot."

"Aye, but I don't look it," said Robin, with a grin; he glanced down at his well-worn green tunic, which had been badly torn in his combat with the beggar. "Yet have no fear—Robin's wit is a match for them all."

The Welshman generously divided his small supply of food in three portions, but Osmund could hardly eat his share of bread for yawning. It was a warm, misty morning and all the grasses and bushes were spread with gossamer threads. Long before the trout were cooked, the boy had curled himself up in the heather and was sound asleep.

There was no rest for Robin Hood, for he well knew that he was engaged in a race against time, with only his shrewd brain to aid him. With his usual impetuosity he had started off armed only with his long-bow and without followers or money. He glanced impatiently at the horizon from time to time, hoping to see the dust raised by the advance of Little-John and his men. The Welshman asked many questions but was chary of answering any in return. Robin watched him without seeming to do so, and noted that though his accoutrements were so dilapidated, the creature's manners were courtly. He excused himself for providing no richer drink than spring water and took out a fair kerchief to wipe the horn after he had quaffed. He had undone his sword-belt for greater ease, and Robin marked that he flung his weapon down carelessly on his right side where he could not readily draw it without bungling.

"By my faith, I'll hazard a guess that 'tis not the bow-string which has hardened thy middle fingers," he cried suddenly.

As he spoke Robin Hood laid his hand playfully on the

scabbard and twitched it out of its owner's reach. It was well that his eyes were on the man's face and that he was as wary as a cat and as quick in movement, for in an instant the Welshman was upon him with drawn dagger.

Robin leaped up and back and parried the blow with the hood which he had taken off for coolness.

"I have eaten your bread," he cried, grasping the little man's wrist in his strong fingers, "and mean you no wrong. But I'm a harpist myself—at times—and think no harm to recognize a brother in the craft."

"Miserable churl—dost rank thyself with me, in whose veins runs the blood of princes?" screamed the dwarf, struggling helplessly in Robin's grip.

"Do not wake the boy," said the forester calmly. "I also may be of quality above my habit, but I make no boast of it, and give you kindly thanks for your courteous hospitality. Sit down again, my lord, and tell me on which day do the folk from either side of the march traffic in Offa's Dyke?"

"Tomorrow," said the Welshman, sulkily belting on his weapon as Robin released him.

"Then if you will come with us, we'll ride forward as soon as the horses are rested, and my boy can sit behind you on the crupper. If my friends have rejoined me I can lend you peaceable garments—if not——"

He broke off—measured the dwarf with his eye and then the sleeping boy.

"Osmund is almost——"

He was going to say 'of Welshman's stature,' but suppressed the phrase as uncivil.

"Do you agree, my Lord Taliesen?" he concluded respectfully, but with a twinkle in his eyes.

"I see thou art an intelligent fellow and not unacquainted with our literature," observed the little man condescendingly.

"Tradition says that Prince Elphin netted the great bard and musician Taliesen from his weir, whereas you have found me by a foul, muddy, Saxon stream! I'll tell thee the tale anon, but I cannot sing it to my harp, as were worthy, for it has been stolen from me by an insolent dog, whose blood shall wash out the injury. My name is Elian-ap-Gruffydd—ap Conan——"

Robin's eyes closed involuntarily as words continued to pour in a torrent from the Welshman's lips. Between dozes, he made the right exclamations of scandalized amazement, pity and horror, as Elian told in more words than the forester would have conceived possible, the tale of his enmity with a Norman baron. To make a very long story short, Elian, who was a noble bard, had won a musical contest and had been rewarded by the late Prince David with the gift of a golden harp. This harp had been stolen by his enemy during a raid, and the Welshman, riding across the march in pursuit, had been attacked by the English, his men had been slain or scattered and he himself had been forced to fly on the English side. The Lord Marchers and their men were on the *qui vive* all along the border, and if taken with arms upon him a Welshman would have short shrift.

"The alternative would be to doff your armour—and return in some other guise," said Robin, amazed that such a simple expedient had not already occurred to the Welshman.

"Thou sayst I am no fighting man," returned Elian, drawing himself up to his full, insignificant height. "But thou knowest nought of the Welshman's spirit of fire! Besides," he added candidly, "I have no acquaintance in this base country who would dare aid me in my present state."

"Say nought against my bonny England," cried the forester, "and I will see you safely back across the border. But I will pray you in return to speak for me to any Welsh chieftain who may purchase this pair of hapless children, and I will undertake to pay thrice the fee they cost him."

Elian replied—with a dozen anecdotes to illustrate his tale—that it was by no means easy to trace folk sold into slavery, especially children. Merchants of such commodities did not work in the open, and were chary of replying to any inquiries.

"Well, then, we'll sleep a couple of hours," interrupted Robin at length, "and ride to the march as soon as may be."

CHAPTER FIVE

THE GROUND BETWEEN the two great earthworks, Wat's Dyke and Offa's Dyke, which wound along the Welsh border, had long been considered neutral territory. The folk of each nation agreed to come here on certain days to barter their wares, and that a perpetual truce should be maintained in this No Man's Land for the convenience of trade. The Welsh brought ewes'-milk cheese, young cattle, strips of salt beef, hogsheads of grease, and kegs of butter. The English had wool, corn and leather to offer, as well as cloth, shoes, armour, and every kind of article beloved of women—combs, scarves, girdles, beauty philtres, and quack remedies.

A Jew or two would be there with a pack on his back, scorned by all, but doing good business nevertheless.

Osmund protested vigorously when Robin informed him that he was to sham sick and lie hid in a hay-mow while the Welshman borrowed his clothes. There was no sign of Little-John, and Robin Hood explained that Elian would be of great use to him at Offa's Dyke, as he—Robin—knew no word of Welsh. They had ridden within half a mile of the dyke and had turned their horses out to graze and seized a few hours' sleep. Also they had eaten well, for Robin had bought provisions and a flask of wine which they shared with their new comrade. The Welshman, who had seemed quite satisfied with a handful of oatcake and a tiny fish and had sought no further meal during the day, now put away such an astonishing amount of food that the others—who had extremely good appetites—were astonished.

"'Tis a habit of our nation," observed Elian complacently as he caught Robin's eye. "In times of shortage we can subsist on next to nothing."

The three comrades were seated on heaps of hay in a loft which formed the upper part of a lonely grange, when Robin announced his plan. The building stood on high pasture-lands, out of sight of any house. A wide extent of country could be seen from it and no one could approach without being marked at a distance. A rough grass track led up to it and meandered away beyond it towards the Welsh border. Osmund was very indignant at his friend's proposal, but the forester was firm.

"I have need of Sir Elian," he said, "and if he rode with me in armour through the English side of the march, he would not stand a dog's chance. The life of any Welshman in arms is forfeit directly he steps over the boundary. 'Tis a cruel law and may date from King Offa's time, for all I know."

"But—but"—Osmund vainly sought for arguments.

"Play the man!" exclaimed Robin. "'Tis thy brother's rescue I am thinking about. This is no merry-making adventure. If Little-John comes up with our party, do you send a man to find me."

Osmund jerked his tunic over his head in sulky silence, and then pulled off his boots of soft leather—much-worn and scratched—and sat down in his shirt.

"Fie, there's a big rent in the tunic, indeed!" exclaimed Elian. "And is there to be no surcoat? I understood the surcoat was now worn in England, whatever."

"Take it or leave it," quoth Robin. "But in courtesy, add a word of thanks to my young friend who has stripped the very clothes off his back for your service."

"The Welsh are a very polite nation," began the little man indignantly, but the forester cut him short.

"However, whatever, and soever!" he cried gaily. "We start forthwith, so you must e'en keep your courteous speeches for the next meeting!"

With that he seized the indignant Sir Elian in his arms and leapt lightly down to the barn floor, disdaining the ladder. Osmund was obliged to press his face into the hay to smother his laughter as Robin ran down the green path between the hay-fields, towing the Welshman after him by the wrist in a way most upsetting to his dignity.

The sight quite restored the boy's good humour, and as soon as the ill-assorted pair were out of view he cast about for an occupation.

Elian's suit of mail lay half-buried in the hay, and what boy could have resisted trying it on? It was dirty, covered with mud and horse hair, but made by a smith who was past-master at his craft. The leg-pieces were chausses of banded mail, and were composed of rows of flat steel rings overlapping each other and sewn on crimson velvet. There was a little tuck between each row, through which ran a cord, so that when the wearer moved the velvet gleamed between the silvery rings. Osmund pulled them on, after a cursory cleaning with bunches of hay. The sleeved tunic, made of the same materials, was too tight, and Osmund was obliged to leave it open in front, almost as wide as the white leather lacing-thong allowed. The inlaid steel cap was a little too large, but Osmund managed to pad it with a bit of hay-rope. It was great fun to be dressed as a knight, and he sought about until he found Sir Elian's sword-belt. The sword was shorter than those used by English knights, who preferred the heavy two-edged blade of Norman design. Elian's scabbard was beautifully inlaid and encrusted with jewels, and the hilt was blazoned with his arms. Osmund girded on the belt, drew the sword and balanced it as his father had taught him. He tried a few sword exercises—thrust and cut, lunge and recover—but his feet slipped in the hay. Perhaps there might be a level space outside where he could practise while still keeping a look-out. Osmund pushed open the wooden shutter which covered the window and gazed round. There was no one to be seen, but far away, at the foot of the slope, a faint spiral of smoke went curling up beyond an oakwood—it might be rising from a farmhouse chimney, or merely from a fire casually kindled by some swineherd in the wood. Why should he not go and see, Osmund asked himself? If Little-John came he would recognize the horses and await his return there, and Osmund was the son of an English knight on English soil, so surely there could be no harm or danger in seeking speech with his countrymen? Sir Elian had repeated the story of his misfortunes as they rode together across the barren moors, which presently gave way to watery pastures where they had crossed the River Dee, south of Chester town. On reflection, Osmund went back to the loft and hid the sword under the dusty hay, left over from the previous summer.

He took off the broad belt too and replaced it with his own green girdle. This was one of his greatest treasures, for it had been given him by Maid Marian herself—she who was now the Lady of Everingham, but who, until last year, had presided as queen of the outlaws who gathered round Robin Hood in Sherwood Forest.

In England the haymakers were at work already, but on these border uplands the grass was still unripe.

He held Elian's steel cap in his hand as he presently went down the green path, with the tall wild-flowers brushing against his mail-clad legs. Most Welshmen, he had heard, were black- or red-haired, so for safety's sake he uncovered his thick, fair hair. Osmund glanced back from time to time, but there was no sign of Little-John and the horses were grazing quietly. Presently he came to the top of a narrow valley or cwm as the Welsh call it—a hollow in the mountain slope. At the farther end a little grey farmhouse nestled in a group of trees. Osmund had a few coins in the silk purse slung round his neck, and he now hauled it up by its twisted cord, extracted a fourpenny bit and went forward with it in his hand.

There was a great barking of dogs as the boy approached the reed-thatched house and he called out to them in Saxon in a friendly tone. A woman came to the door but rushed in again when she saw that the stranger wore armour. Two men came running from the barn with flails in their hands, which they raised threateningly. Osmund called out again.

"Good morrow, friends! I am alone and unarmed!"

He held up his hands as Elian had done and began to feel that he had been very foolish. Tales of border lawlessness and cruelty crowded into his mind, but he forced himself to walk forward.

"I am page to an English knight," he called. "And seek but to buy bread and cheese, for my lord has gone away and left me unprovided."

"He speaks not like a Welshman," said one of the men, lowering his flail.

"Why, 'tis but a boy," cried a girl's voice, and a buxom milkmaid came out of the byre with a wooden pail of milk on her arm. "Why, what's all the pother about? I'll wager the fellow has but lost his way to the fairing-grounds."

"Indeed, damsel, you say truly," Osmund answered for himself. He spoke very politely, and though the milkmaid shouted with laughter at being addressed like a 'gentle,' she was pleased all the same.

"Thou'rt welcome to break thy fast and keep thy four-penny," she went on as Osmund made his request. "We look not so closely to the store but that we can spare bite and sup to a wayfarer. Come, sit you on the bench at the dairy door and tell me who thy master is while I turn my cheeses."

She spoke a strange dialect, which Osmund could only partly understand, for there were words of Danish origin mixed with the Saxon. He was unwilling to talk of himself, for though he might truly call himself page to a knight, he did not wish to give away further information to strangers. The milkmaid, however, was quite ready to talk herself—she told him that she was the farmer's daughter and that her father had gone to sell some lambs at the Dyke Fair—she was just handing a heavy slice of barley bread and cheese to the boy, when one of the men drew near.

"Doll, take heed! Best send the brat packing! You'll have the whole swarm down upon us else," he muttered.

Sir Elian had talked about the country folk coming out like a swarm of bees: Osmund pricked up his ears.

"My master does not come from these parts," he said. "He is a great man in the Eastern Counties, and has but gone to look at the fair out of curiosity. He is a stranger from Yorkshire."

"Well, we want no strangers here," persisted the man. "So begone, Sir Page, before the dogs are loosed at your heels."

Doll tossed her head:

"'Tis I who give orders here," she declared, "and I say the lad shall sit and eat and pass the time for me. Go about your business, Tom ploughman, and leave me to manage mine."

"You were glad enough to call for my protection when you thought the Welsh were coming t'other day," retorted the man. "And there's a Welshman abroad yet, and likely to be a fierce one, too."

"But surely you are five or six miles from the border here?" cried Osmund.

"Scarce one; and the Welsh will go twenty or more—curse them—to get our cattle," said Doll. "And our young men match them! There's bad blood in these parts ever since the King's army was cut to pieces in grandfather's time. Over there,

'twas—where the Welsh have a stronghold above the Dee—
Ewloe Castle, they call it."

"But surely English folk have no need to raid Welsh cattle?"
asked Osmund. "I've always thought the Lord Marchers kept
stern rule here."

"Aye, but the lads was vexed, see you. The Welsh have been
crowing ever since the Victory of Ewloe, as they call it—and the
ale had gone round too often at the Midsummer Feast. However
'twas, the lads went across the dyke on a dark night and did
some mischief, I believe, and carried off some of the Welshmen's gear——"

"And broke the Taffies' heads when they came after 'em," put
in the hind with a grin.

"There was three men killed," said the girl. "But they made
less stir over that than over a fiddle, or harp, or some such thing
as the lads ran off with for a marlock. I would it were safe back,
for I know the Welsh better than these folk do—they put their
pride above the lives of men, and will have vengeance."

Osmund had emptied the wooden bowl of milk and eaten a
good portion of bread and cheese during this discourse.

"Farewell, kind damsel," he said, putting on his steel cap in
order to doff it as he got up. "And here, churl, is fourpence to
mend thy manners to strangers."

He tossed the battered silver coin to the labourer, who
stood rubbing his beard and staring uncertainly at him, and
then walked out of the yard with all the dignity he could muster.

He had just passed the angle of the lane when he heard running footsteps crossing the field on his left.

A moment later there was a rustling in the hedge, the untrimmed growths of hazel and wild-rose were parted and Doll's
large, round, rosy face peered through.

"Hist! Quiet now!" she whispered, and paused to look over
her shoulder.

HE GAZED ANXIOUSLY AT HER BROAD, HONEST FACE AND THEN
CLAMBERED UP THE BANK

(*See page* 40)

Osmund halted and looked round too. The lane was empty, but he heard one of the horses neigh far above at the grange.

"Maybe I'm wrong," said Doll, in a hoarse, reedy whisper. "But maybe it was the Welsh harp you had in your mind when you came to our place?"

"The Welsh harp!" repeated Osmund eagerly. "No—yes—wait a minute, Doll." He gazed anxiously at her broad, honest face, and then clambered up the bank. "Listen, the Welsh hold my young brother and sister prisoners—and if only I could lay hands on the harp I'd have something to bargain with."

"You must promise to give it back though, if I tell you where it is hid—and not bring the Welsh seeking it," she insisted. "You must swear you'll not bring the Welsh about our ears."

"I promise, as I'm a Christian," declared Osmund.

He stretched his head upwards among the green leaves. Doll bent down and whispered:

"In the monks' rush-stack at Haordin Castle."

"But where *is* Haordin?" demanded Osmund.

There was no answer. The branches flew up again as Doll jumped down into the field. Someone was coming along the mountain track—a huge man dressed in green. He walked bent in two and kept moving from one hedgerow to the other, grumbling and exclaiming all the time as he hurried along.

"Little-John!" shouted Osmund joyfully.

CHAPTER SIX

LITTLE-JOHN returned Osmund's greeting with equal heartiness. He stood upright, his great arms stretched from hedge to hedge.

"Well met, Blackbird, well met! Beshrew me if Robin hath not forgotten how to lay a patteran! My back is nearly broken searching for signs of his track—but where is he, and what news? Why, I scarce knew you in yon mailed gear!"

Osmund made no mention of Elian's harp as they went back up the hill. Honest Little-John was not as fine-witted as his friend and comrade Robin Hood, and Osmund felt that the affair must be carefully handled.

Little-John and his men were very tired—and Osmund suggested that he should go and find Robin, while they took a little rest. The Castle men-at-arms were anxious to accompany their young master, but he declared that he was safer alone. He promised faithfully not to approach the Welsh side of the earthwork, and then, mounting his horse, cantered down the hill and into the bridle-track which led to Offa's Dyke. As he drew near he could hear the lowing of cattle and the shouts of the vendors, and now and then a snatch of music. The road was churned into mud and marked with the feet of sheep and unshod country horses. Osmund thought it prudent to turn aside and tie up his steed in a little wood before he plunged into the throng.

Welsh and English voices vied with each other, frightened heifers charged through the crowds, tumblers beat drums to attract attention to their show, and earnest housewives bargained for Welsh cheeses and hams. The fair, though not large, was so animated and noisy that Osmund almost despaired of finding his friend. As he passed anxiously about from group to group, he was more closely remarked than he himself was aware of.

The Welsh, both gentle and simple, shaved the hair on their faces, save that on the upper lip. All young men, even nobles, went barefoot, and wore only a light tunic to the knee and a mantle of thin silk or coarse homespun according to their quality. They were easily distinguishable among the bearded English peasantry, and first one man began to follow Osmund, then another joined him, and presently five or six moved after him.

Osmund began to feel very hot and uncomfortable. He turned round and spoke to the best-dressed of the group in English: the man responded in vehement Welsh, which, of course, Osmund could not understand. He endeavoured to turn back towards the English side of the dyke, but immediately the Welshmen ringed him round and began to hustle him in the opposite direction.

"Robin! Robin! Come to my help!" shouted Osmund, resisting as best he could. No doubt the men had recognized the little Welshman's armour. "Sir Elian, Sir Elian, Sir Elian!" he now called. "Does any Englishman here speak Welsh? Will no one explain for me?"

Two or three stout English drovers hurried up, staves in hand; the Welshmen paused, puzzled by Osmund's cries for the very man whom they imagined he had robbed, if not murdered. Osmund hardly knew how to explain the situation without bringing the dwarf knight into danger, but while he struggled and stammered, Robin Hood came upon the scene, and with a thrust or two of his powerful arms passed through the crowd and stood at Osmund's side. The Welsh, seeing themselves hopelessly outnumbered, released him, and running into the bushes which flanked the base of Offa's Dyke, they were out of sight in a moment, seeming to melt into the landscape like running deer.

"How now, Osmund, what do you here?" inquired the forester gravely. "I thank you, friends, for your timely help," he added to the drovers. "This page belongs to a patron of mine and has taken French leave to follow me, as the archers say."

"It is ill meddling with the Welsh, though," said one drover. "They have been hardly treated in the past and are of vengeful nature. That young knave of thine might well have caused a riot."

They hurried back to their beasts and Robin stood still, looking sternly at Osmund.

"Little-John has come," said the boy. "I never thought the armour would be recognized, Robin. Our folk are resting at the grange, for they are mighty weary, and you did not forbid me to follow you—so I came."

"Blackbird, thou must learn to obey the wish as well as the word, else canst thou not be counted a member of our fellowship," quoth the forester. "Come, we must find Elian, who is lingering at the soothsayer's booth. So far we have discovered nothing."

"Is there no news of Hild and Eadgar?" asked Osmund anxiously.

Robin Hood shook his head.

This was a grievous disappointment. Osmund's faith in his friend was so great that he had hitherto had no real fear as to the final outcome. But if Robin Hood, the invincible, had failed to track the slavers, or if they had vanished with their prey across the lawless Welsh border, what hope was left? It was but a day's ride to the sea, and were there not always Irish pirates cruising off the coast of Wales, ready to aid evil-doers for a share in the booty?

"They tell me the border barons will not raise a finger to help any wrong," went on Robin Hood. "Their following is greatly weakened by the King's French war, and men are scarcely to be had to reap the corn, archers' wages are so high-risen. So I am of a mind——"

He paused, looking down at Osmund with that laughing light in his eyes which always betokened a dangerous errand.

"I'll come too!" said Osmund quickly.

"And so thou shalt," agreed the forester approvingly. A brave spirit pleased him, and he was of opinion that a likely youth could not serve his apprenticeship to perilous deeds too early. Maid Marian might not have agreed with him, and it was very certain that the Lady Etheldreda would not have done so. But Robin felt confident that his own strength, shrewdness and proficiency in arms would serve to preserve the boy's life, and he recked little of difficulties and perils which fell short of death itself.

"It was a foolish notion to don the Welshman's armour, Blackbird," said Robin Hood. "But I fear thou takest after me and art inclined to leap before looking. Seest thou, these Welshmen are ticklish as to points of honour and so forth—they are easily offended."

"They don't like being carried off by force, in fact," rejoined Osmund slyly.

"Well, it seems I cannot blame you without blaming myself," cried Robin Hood cheerfully. "Between us we have offended the goblin knight, and he is not disposed to do more to help us. He advises us to apply direct to the Prince, a noble and most gracious youth, by his telling and his special patron."

"Then Sir Elian will plead our cause himself?" exclaimed Osmund hopefully.

But the forester shook his head. "That is just what he will not do. Either the man is just drawing the long-bow about his noble lineage and grand acquaintance or else——"

"Or else what, good Master Robin?"

"Or else he has given the Prince a cause of anger against him. I am mighty unlearned in these ways, Osmund, so sit down on this knoll and let us divide this gingerbread cake while you tell me all you know about the Princes and governance of Wales."

"Oh, that we had Eadgar here!" said the boy, and then he kept silence for a moment while he wondered anxiously in what plight poor Eadgar and Hild might be at this very moment. It seemed as though they were wasting time, yet he knew that Robin Hood's ways were to be trusted and he racked his brains as to what he knew.

"The Welsh are always at war among themselves, I've heard," he said at last. "They had a great prince called Owen who ruled over them all, but he died ages ago—before our King came to the throne."

"More than five years ago then?" said Robin, smiling.

"Nay, when my father was a little boy—at least twenty-five years ago. And ever since all the Welsh princes have been fighting each other and the Lord Marchers."

"H'm—difficult to keep out of brawls if you're a marcher," commented the forester. "If you are friendly with your Welsh neighbour his enemies attack you, and if you are unfriendly he attacks you himself! Who is King of Wales now?"

"They don't have a king—they just have princes—and the Prince of Gwynedd is their overlord. He has just succeeded to the throne, and he is quite, quite young—only sixteen or seventeen. Wido had a song about him."

"A green sapling makes an uncertain shot; he's over-young," said Robin. "What else?"

"That is all I know," confessed Osmund, "except that the Welsh are always raiding across the border, and, of course, the English raid back——"

"And perhaps the other way about," interrupted Robin, "But go on."

"A girl at the farm over yonder told me that in this last raid—at Sir Elian's place, I suppose, a harp had been stolen—she said the Welsh would set the whole country in a blaze for a mere harp."

"Easy to be seen thou art no minstrel! But I have a notion—above all things we have time to beat. Maybe that was why Elian refused to go to his Prince. What was it he said about the harp? Oh, plague upon it, but the fool's long tales made me slumber."

"He said that a bard must never part with the harp which is the Prince's gift," repeated Osmund; "and so I thought if we could find the harp we would have something to bargain with—but if we can't save Hild and Eadgar soon, they may be carried off to Ireland——"

Robin Hood gave his young friend a playful blow which sent him rolling on the grass.

"Aye, but you foolish fellow, we're only *waiting* for a harp!" he declared. "Where said the girl that the instrument lay hid?"

"In the monks' rush-stack at Haordin Castle," repeated Osmund. "But how shall we find that?"

"By using our wits, to be sure! For it will be a brave shot in our quiver. Ride quickly to the grange—doff that suit of mail, and if Elian has not yet sent back thy tunic take Much's, and push the overflow under thy belt. Tell Tuck I have need of his friar's gown, and bid them all await my coming——"

"When—where?" asked Osmund breathlessly.

Robin Hood reflected for a moment.

"Wherever they find good hunting," he decided carelessly at length. "They must keep a man on watch at the grange, so that I can find them if need arise. But you and I will try peaceful methods first. Hold a moment, Blackbird!"

Osmund had already sprung up.

"Bid Little-John brew a mess of the brown moss that clings about the roots of heather—and say he must put in lumps of pine gum and make a thick mixture, strong enough to dye gold. And now begone, for I must find Elian and make some inquiries ere we get to business."

There were a dozen questions at the tip of Osmund's tongue, but he only asked:

"Is there anything more, Master Robin? And will the Merry Men take your orders from my mouth?"

"Well thought of! Show them this." The forester stooped and plucked a long grass-blade, which he wound in a knot about two leaves which he took from his pouch.

"Was it by such a sign that Little-John and our folk followed you hither?" inquired Osmund.

"Ask no question to which you can find the answer yourself— that is a greenwood law," returned Robin. "You know very well we of the greenwood have each a patteran like the gipsy folk, and leave a sign when we travel by which our friends may follow us. Now haste away, but do not run in sight of the folk or they will take thee for a thief."

Osmund followed this advice, but nevertheless made good speed. He had fully hoped to get to the knoll before Robin Hood's return, but as he came out of the bushes and advanced sideways down the steep grassy slope of the earthwork, he saw his friend's figure seated on the same spot as though he had never moved.

"Little-John is waiting in the copse with the two best horses," announced Osmund, panting a little as he came up the mound.

"Elian has fled," said Robin. "No doubt he was afraid when his men began to hustle you. I doubt he won't send his folk to return thy tunic, either."

"There has been no sign of them yet," agreed Osmund. "Little-John is monstrous discontent, and he bid me say——"

"I can guess the whole tale, but we have no time to listen to it. Hark ye, Osmund, 'tis a big pity that we know no Welsh, but fortune serves us, nevertheless. I have fallen in with some of the Welsh Prince's men, who were buying wine and provisions for his table. And we'll e'en follow them back to his Court tonight—at least, the harper and his boy will."

"And will the harper be blind, Master Robin?"

"Nay, lad, this time the harper has need of his eyes."

"And where are we going now?" inquired Osmund.

He was forced to adopt a sort of trotting pace, for the forester was covering the ground with huge strides, as he passed rapidly through the crowd and hastened towards the group of ash trees where Little-John was awaiting them.

"I'll tell you when I know myself," answered Robin cheerfully.

CHAPTER SEVEN

OSMUND COULD not restrain his mirth as he watched Robin Hood endeavouring to fold Friar Tuck's immense frock about his tall, sinewy frame. Tuck had once spent a few penitential months as porter to a monastery, and had fled thence wearing the garment which had been bestowed upon him in all charity. He had an absurd fondness for it—patched and ragged though it was—and refused to part from it. Only Robin's command could have induced him even to lend it for a few hours.

The whilom outlaw, serious for once, struggled to arrange the vast folds, and then girded himself with the worn leather belt, in which he drilled a new hole with his knife, tucking in the long end.

"Well, lad? With that black hood I have bought me, shall I not pass as a brother?"

"Perhaps—at a goodly distance," agreed Osmund. "A monk would have a rosary in his belt—not a hunting-knife, though."

"This is a knife for cutting rushes," declared Robin with a grin. "But perhaps a hook were better. We'll buy one as we go along."

So saying, he stuck his knife into his stocking and sprang upon his horse. Osmund mounted the other and they moved cautiously to the edge of the thicket.

"We'll go back to the Fair and choose a hook," said Robin.

"And mind you look lowly and humble, Blackbird, as befits a youth trained in the cloister."

He touched his horse with his heel and cantered along the top of the embankment until he came to a cattle-track slanting down it. A little below them in the bright sunshine were a couple of very beautiful horses of that noble Spanish breed introduced into the border country by the famous Norman, Robert of Belesme, the builder of a score of strongholds on Welsh land. The horse couper kept them disdainfully apart from the thick-set country steeds, and though many came to admire, there seemed to be no buyers.

The men saluted the shabby monk respectfully.

"I fear this fair will hardly attract folk of sufficient quality to buy your fine beasts," said Robin, speaking in a feigned voice which made Osmund jump.

"If truth be told, we've had no offer as yet, brother," returned the dealer.

Robin pulled a few coins from his pouch and bade Osmund go and buy a reaping-knife such as was used for gathering rushes. When he returned, Robin was still talking to the horse-dealers; he kept his serious expression and shook his head mournfully from time to time, but when Osmund came within earshot, he found the conversation did not match the expression at all.

"I'll look for thee at next Martinmas and we'll have a merry time," Robin was saying. "But just now I have need of those two horses—if they are as good as they look, which, indeed, I think they are, the price is not too high. Gold I have none for the moment, but meet me at the church yonder—I see the tower above the elm-trees—tonight at six, and I'll come purse in hand."

"What do we now?" asked Osmund.

"Why, gather rushes, to be sure," rejoined Robin.

He turned his horse's head and rode up the dyke again. Osmund checked his pace in passing the Spanish horses. They were stamping their slender feet at the flies, tossing their proud little heads and switching their long, silky tails. Osmund had never in his life bestridden such a creature, and, of course, longed to do so.

Robin beguiled the way by instructing Osmund on how to lay a 'patteran'; he had acquired the art from the gipsies, each of whom have a personal and a tribal patteran, which consists in twisting certain leaves and grasses together and laying them under the hedge at intervals so as to form a trail which only the initiated can find and follow.

They rode over pasture-land for some way till Robin said: "We'll strike into the wood here, Blackbird, and I'll ride first. Look, yonder flies the flag on the Castle turret!"

Osmund's eyes followed Robin's pointing finger, and he saw the warm, red sandstone of the Castle wall rising through trees high above them. The country they had traversed formed a series of wooded ridges, with marshy valleys between. There were many streams, and now, as they halted their horses, the sound of running water filled the air. The Castle stood on an artificial eminence which crowned a cone-shaped hillock. Robin Hood rode down through the untrimmed oakwoods, crossing some abandoned out-works fast falling into decay. At the bottom of the ferny slope ran a wide, sluggish stream, broadening here and there into long pools.

"A good place for water-fowl," quoth Robin. "And there are certainly rushes a-plenty. If thou canst see the rush-stack before I do, Blackbird, I'll give thee a silver penny."

There was no one about, and they went on, glancing keenly from side to side. Osmund was the first to call out that he saw swathes of cut rushes drying on the grass. Robin had seen them some minutes earlier, but he said nothing, and presently dismounted and tied his horse to a tree. A moment later he made an exclamation of annoyance and pointed to the stack on the further side of the stream.

"Hide the knife," he said peremptorily. "No, give it to me."

"LOOK, YONDER FLIES THE FLAG ON THE CASTLE TURRET!"

(See page 53)

Osmund watched the long chopper disappear through the hole in Friar Tuck's gown—rent wider for the purpose—and waited orders in silence.

"Yesterday thou wert careless enough to lose the reaping-knife," announced the forester severely, "and holy poverty demands that we find our tool again. It may even have been built into the rush-stack, for I call to mind that thou hadst it in hand when we laid on the last sheaf. Truss up thy chausses—take off thy shoes, and we'll e'en ford the stream and search for it."

The bottom of the stream was deep in mud, and Osmund was obliged to clutch the man's strong arm as he slipped and stumbled in the water. They were hailed by a dissipated-looking man-at-arms with a hawk on his wrist as they scrambled up the opposite bank. The mock-friar shouted up the story of the reaping-knife, and the other bawled down his advice to give the boy a sound thrashing. He watched for a moment to see if the brother intended to put his counsel into immediate execution, but seeing the pair merely begin their work at the stack he strolled off and took no more interest.

In a very few minutes Osmund's fingers touched something hard and then a melancholy, muted note sounded as he grazed a harp-string. Robin drew out the knife, and also a coil of rope with which he bound up a large bundle of rush sheaves with the harp in the centre.

"We'll carry it between us," he said. "Pull up the reeds on thy side to cover that gleam of gold." He rebuilt the stack swiftly and they hastened back across the water. When the horses were reached Robin slung the bundle across his back, with a great fringe of rushes sticking up over his head.

CHAPTER EIGHT

THE RETURN JOURNEY to the dyke was very wearisome. Though it was downhill the going was bad, and the horses tripped and stumbled continually. Osmund was terribly hungry: the sun was going down and he could not help hoping that Little-John would have a meal ready for them and that they would be able to sleep in the hay-mow before riding further. But he was determined to utter no complaint.

Little-John met them half a mile below the grange. He was full of complaints and discontent, and implored Robin Hood to let him take part in the adventure. But Robin was adamant.

"I have other work for you to do," he declared. "For, look you, as Elian would say, I believe we can spit two birds with one bolt."

"Which two birds?" inquired Little-John. "Speak plain words, as befits an honest yeoman," exclaimed John. "For truly I am in no mood to follow flights of fancy."

"First, then, we must rescue Eadgar and the little maid, secondly, we must punish the slavers; and I want you to watch for them at this side of the border."

"It seems we are to be at the beck and call of every brat in the country," grumbled John, trying to force his good-humoured features into a scowl.

"Blackbird and I will undertake to find the captives, and you, Little-John, must trace and punish the slavers," Robin ordered. "Is the beggar still in our company?"

"He is up above at the grange, and anxious to join our band."

"We will try him first—is he trusty, think you? Would he serve to get speech with the slavers in case they have already sold their prisoners?"

"H'm, that is a ticklish errand—one I had best undertake myself," said John, his face clearing at the idea of a dangerous adventure. "And hark ye, Robin—it will be strange if Maid Marian be not soon upon thy track."

"Just what I think," agreed Robin. "We have no time to lose. Have you any money upon you, friend? I have need of a score of gold pieces."

"The beggar's wallet is well-lined," said John, coolly. "And I brought it along—was not that well thought of?"

"So that accounts for your bruised lip and swollen nose," cried Robin, much amused. "Cut a tally stick, Little-John, and Osmund shall count the coins. As the fellow is only a novice— so to speak—we must be prepared to hand him back his purse, if he leaves our company."

While he was talking, Robin Hood had unbound the big bundle of rushes and disclosed a small golden harp. He plucked the strings critically and then, taking from John a smoking pot of some sticky, dark compound, he proceeded to dab it all over the frame of the instrument until every glint of gold was hidden.

"'Tis real gold, not gold-leaf," declared Little-John admiringly. "And I doubt if the dye will ever stick to it, though I put in the pine-gum as you bid me."

"It will dry in half-an-hour," declared Robin. "And I'll go bail thou hast a slice or two of venison frying for us, which we can eat while we wait."

He sniffed the air, and then strode behind a thick bush where a low wood fire was burning, and thin collops of meat were frizzling on wooden skewers on the hot stones in the centre. A leather bottle of wine hung from an adjacent bough.

Little-John produced flat loaves, like large bread-buns, which were used both for plate and nourishment. The custom was to cut your loaf in two with the knife which everyone carried, scoop out the lower portion and lay on it a copious helping of meat and gravy. Then, having eaten one's meat—throwing any bits of bone or gristle which it might contain under the table—one finished up by eating the 'plate' itself, now agreeably soaked with gravy.

On this occasion the three friends sat down close to the fire, slit their loaves in two and helped themselves by digging the points of their knives into the sizzling collops. It was the best meal Osmund had had for three days, and he did ample justice to it. Robin Hood managed to dispose of two collops to Osmund's one, and John twitted him with having put on Friar Tuck's appetite at the same time as his frock. Robin retorted with one of his playful blows which made even the gigantic Little-John reel. He wasted no time on words, but rose directly he had finished eating, pulled off his monkish disguise and slung the harp across his back.

"Take my horse," he said then. "Ride down to the market and buy a couple of gay cloaks and a pink feather for Osmund's cap. Thou'lt meet us on the road that goes from the church yonder into Wales."

Little-John did his commission well and the horse-coupers were prompt at the tryst. The beggar's purse was considerably lightened as Robin paid without bargaining. The 'luck-penny' which the dealer handed back Robin tossed to the stable-boy, and springing into the saddle, he rode gaily away. No one could have recognized the toil-worn monk and his henchman in the somewhat raffish-looking pair who rode over the bridge into Wales a few minutes later. They bestrode princely horses and their mantles vied with the rainbow, but anyone could mark mud-stained hose and worn sleeves protruding from under the silken folds.

"Followers of the gay science," said the folk, looking after them. Anyone could have guessed them to be travelling gleemen without even seeing the harp.

Robin Hood led the way at a brisk pace for about five miles, then he pulled up and looked keenly about him. They had just reached the top of a long rise and were surrounded by bleak moorland, with patches of pasture broken by marshy pools and groups of wind-dashed thorn-trees. A stormy sunset flamed in yellow and orange to their right and behind, the border hills, magnified by the evening mist, showed rose-coloured where the light shone on sandstone and wet, brown bracken.

Osmund insensibly drew closer to his leader and Robin's long-bow, which he was carrying, rattled, and made his horse so restive that he could hardly control it.

"What are we waiting for, Master Robin? Steady! Whoa there, stand!" cried Osmund breathlessly.

Robin made a queer sound—a low, prolonged whistle and then said a string of still queerer words in a strange, chanting tone.

The restless horse stood quite still, trembling a little and pricking its ears.

"We're waiting for the retinue of the Prince of Gwynedd. They were down at the fair buying provisions, and their lord is camped somewhere about fifteen miles off. He is the head Prince, as you told me very truly, and the Prince of Powys has done him homage, but he has an uncle at Oswaldstree that he is none too sure of, and a cousin in the next contref or commote, or whatever they call it—Merry something—hark, I hear horses!"

"What about the cousin?" queried Osmund.

"Well, it seems he thinks he has a chance of being overlord himself and is in no hurry to do homage to his kinsman."

"Oh," said Osmund.

It all sounded very complicated and warlike. The popular impression of the Welsh was that they were always murdering each other in family feuds, and there were horrid stories of their cruelties. But then there were horrid stories about English cruelties too! King Henry put child hostages to death and Prince John starved his enemies in underground dungeons.

"What language was that in which you spoke to the horses?" he asked, trying to make his voice sound quite casual and self-assured.

"Fairy language—or phœnician, as they call it in Ireland," rejoined his friend. "I learnt it from the gipsies. Now, when these people come up, make your horse curvet—show him to advantage."

The wet road twisted away behind them like a grey snake, and Osmund could see no one, nor hear a sound save the sharp stabbing note of flitting moorland finches. But a few minutes after Robin had spoken a little procession of men and laden ponies came into view, laboriously climbing the hill.

Two riders, armed with light lances, detached themselves from the main body and advanced at a rapid trot. They drew rein when they reached Robin Hood and his companion and saluted courteously, calling some question in Welsh.

Robin returned the salute with studied grace.

"Alas, I have no Welsh," he said. "But I journey to the court of the noble Llewelyn, to seek a boon, offer a gift and sing a lay."

"The Prince would love you better if you put the last first," answered one of the men in a sing-song tone. He was nicknamed 'the Sassenach' on account of his proficiency in the language. "But he is always glad to greet a fellow-musician, therefore, I pray you, ride on in our company."

The Welshmen were young and ill-mounted, and their glances kept returning admiringly to the strangers' horses.

"Those are no merlins from Llanfyllin horse-fair," remarked Gwyllim Sassenach. "Where got you those choice bits of horse-flesh, Master Harper?"

"By honest purchase," returned Robin. "But truly they are over-fine for a poor minstrel and his boy—they are more meet for a prince."

"I thought Merlin was a Welsh prophet," put in Osmund. "Or did you mean the hawk—" He added hastily: "Fair sir," realizing that a gleeman's servant would be unlikely to take part in the conversation unbidden, as a knight's son might do.

"Nay, the merlin is a special breed of pony, strong and handsome little beasts fit for mountain-riding."

"Like yours?" suggested Osmund.

"Yes, indeed, like mine," repeated the Sassenach, but he sighed and cast envious looks at the Spanish horses.

Presently a wall of mountains came into view on the left, while the ground fell away in front, and Gwyllim led the way across a wild, untracked moor.

"The main way goes by a steep pass, or notch, as we call it, down the mountain," explained the Welshman. "But as our beasts are heavy-laden we shall strike across by the oak woods, avoiding the defile—and pass out of Powysland," he added in a lower tone.

He called something to his companion, who pressed forward and led the way over country which Osmund had never seen matched save in nightmare sleep. Now they were splashing through a boggy morass, where the Spanish horses plunged and slithered and nearly unseated at least one of their riders. A few minutes later the sumpter-ponies, who were shod, were striking sparks out of the flinty ridges of rock which broke through the thin crust of earth. Next, in the failing light, there was a woodland valley to be traversed, and Robin groaned, fearing their precious mounts would do themselves a mischief.

"Hold hard! Master Sassenach," he cried. "This may be good merlin country, but beshrew me if it will not maim a gift for a prince!"

"Fearest thou to follow us? Is it as my comrades say, then, art thou a spy?" exclaimed Sassenach, pulling up.

In a moment the two strangers were surrounded by a ring of angry faces, and the dying light glittered on the long knives which every man had drawn from his stocking.

"My master is no spy," cried Osmund indignantly. "He is a——"

"Harmless musician, seeking his fortune," interrupted Robin. "Take my weapons if you will, but in honesty admit that I am only in your company by your own invitation. In my country we fling not evil words at our guests."

This remark cut Gwyllim to the soul. If there is one thing upon which a Welshman prides himself more than another it is in courtesy to strangers.

"I crave your pardon most humbly," exclaimed the young man, crimsoning down to the collar of his scarlet mantle. He poured forth some excited phrases in Welsh, and then leaping to the ground he begged Robin's leave to lead his horse himself until they should regain a road.

As they wound their way along the narrow track Robin Hood began to sing, half under his breath.

"Childe Roland to the dark tower came——"

Osmund felt an eerie sensation rush through him. The wind howled down the valley, and as they at length emerged from the shadow of the trees a cold rainstorm dashed against their faces.

CHAPTER NINE

THE WELSH WERE not as yet great castle builders, they preferred the ancient hall, presided over by the tribal chief. Their favourite methods of warfare were by swift attack or by ambush—sitting down for three or four months to starve out a fortress did not appeal to them in the least.

As the travellers drew near the dwelling where the young Prince was staying, they could see its long outline high on the hillside. A strong column of smoke rose above the roof and soft, ruddy light streamed from the wide-open doors.

"You know our custom, doubtless," said Gwyllim, riding up to Robin Hood. "The door is always open to the guest, and when he comes in the maidens of the house will hasten forward to offer him water to wash his feet. If he refuses, it is a sign that he is journeying farther that night, but if he accepts it means that he wishes to stay."

"I thank you, fair sir," replied Robin, "and will accept the Prince's hospitality in the generous spirit in which he offers it."

"Any Welsh house would do the same, were it but a wattle hut," returned the other proudly.

They toiled up the ascent, and Osmund was surprised to find that there was no attempt at cultivation in the neighbourhood of the hall—no garth, nor ploughed fields, only wild pasture thickly studded with clumps of wild-rose and seedling thorns. As they drew near the door four or five youths ran out to take their horses, while maidens in garments of thin silk came to the doorway to light them in with torches. Gwyllim had hurried on ahead and had already dismounted, he was endeavouring to talk two languages at once—to introduce the strangers, to bid them welcome, and to tell the news he had gleaned during the day, all at the same time.

The apartment into which they entered reminded Osmund of nothing so much as the abbey tithe-barn. Clouds of smoke from the large wood fire in the middle, hung about the roof, making it look higher than it actually was. The vast space was full of people, some at chess, some eating and drinking, some playing with beautiful hounds—Osmund counted ten or twelve of these—and some calmly sleeping on the broad bench which ran all round the wall.

The maidens led the strangers in courteously by the hand, brought seats for them—stools with low arms and no backs—and offered them water for their feet, which they duly accepted. One girl wheeled up a large harp and prepared to entertain the new guests with music and song, a second gracefully presented a gilded horn, filled to the brim with wine, and a third knelt down to unlace the travellers' muddy buskins.

Robin would have protested had he not been afraid his action would be misunderstood, but Osmund saved his embarrassment by plumping down on the floor, ducking his head in what was intended for a polite salute to the kneeling maiden, and undoing Robin's buskins himself.

"'Tis my duty to serve my master," he observed.

To his surprise the girl answered him in English, though with a pretty lilt in her tones which betrayed her origin.

"In Gwynedd we think no shame to serve a guest, be he gentle or simple."

"A right noble custom," cried Robin, giving Osmund a push with his knee as a warning that he was to be discreet. "Pray tell me, is the most noble Llewelyn in residence, fair maiden? For we have ridden over the border to beg a boon which admits no delay."

"My cousin is but now returned from hunting," said she. "And he will soon be here to bid you welcome. Supper will be served in less than half an hour, but if you be hungry, food shall be brought forthwith."

"We'll await supper, I thank you," said Robin. "But meanwhile I would gladly empty this horn to the glorious customs of ancient Wales."

While Robin drank, Osmund washed and dried his feet and fitted on a beautiful pair of deerskin shoes from the selection which the girl brought him.

"Do let me do your feet," she whispered to him. "And then I can stay and talk to you. Otherwise I shall be sent away and you will be entertained by Eluned and Essylt."

"All right—you pour out the water," agreed Osmund. "How did you learn to speak English so well? Have you talked to any other English boy lately?"

"What a strange question!" said she.

Osmund looked up eagerly. The girl was quite young—not very much older than himself, and very pretty.

"I did not mean to be over-curious or rude," he urged. "But we are in search of my brother and sister, who have been carried off by slavers into Wales, and I hoped—I wondered—if you could have seen them?"

"We can't talk now," she answered, hastily dragging a shoe on to his foot. "But I'll send my brother Rhun to you at supper. My name is Gwenllian and that is my sister Eluned at the harp."

The lady with the drinking-horn made her a sign and Gwenllian rose immediately and beckoned a serf-woman to remove the basin. She herself gathered up the towel and went out of the room by a curtained doorway behind the dais at the far end.

Servants now began to set up trestle tables with long oak benches on either side and the Welsh took their places, the better-born in groups of three, and the others in indiscriminate rows. When the huge dishes of smoking meat were carried in, the curtains parted behind the dais and a young man of striking beauty came in and uttered some courteous phrase of greeting.

Osmund had posted himself behind Robin Hood in the customary position of a page, but the Prince observed this and sent one of his own suite to lead him to a seat. There were evidently many other guests besides the Harper and his boy, and the Prince and members of his family waited on some themselves and kept issuing orders for the care and comfort of all. They walked round the hall, seeing that everyone was served, speaking kindly welcome to high and low and making sure that all wants were attended to before they withdrew to the dais and began their own meal.

Meanwhile musicians sang, played, cracked jokes and asked riddles which provoked shouts of laughter. Osmund's neighbours spoke only Welsh, so he could hold no conversation with them, and presently turned his attention to Llewelyn. The Prince was about eighteen years old at this time. He was tall and well-developed, with a broad brow and dark, chestnut hair cut below the ears, instead of flowing to the shoulders according to the new fashion. His eyes were keen and penetrating, set rather deep, under straight, finely pencilled brows: at first sight he might be set down as a fighter, at a second glance divined to be a dreamer: in fact, brain and body were equally matched in this noblest of Welshmen. A garland of golden oakleaves fitted closely round his head and he wore a wide-sleeved tunic, with a woven border of green and gold.

Osmund watched, fascinated, and was startled when a voice suddenly whispered in his ear:

"I am Rhun."

A boy stepped over the bench and sat down beside him.

"Are you a harper, too?" he inquired. "The Prince is going to ask your father to play as soon as supper is finished."

"He is not my father," began Osmund—and stopped abruptly.

"I have been sent to entertain you and bid you welcome," went on the Welsh boy. "My sister tells me you have come to look for a lost brother. What is he like? Because yesterday we saw some men from Meirionydd—they are wild, fierce folk from the mountains, and their overlord has not yet done homage to Llewelyn as he ought to do——"

"Well, go on!" urged Osmund breathlessly.

"They had some folk with them, bound—a youth and maiden—and they said they were villeins who had run away—but we don't have villeins in Wales."

"Eadgar is a little taller than me and dark and much more Norman-looking," declared Osmund. "He has a curved nose——"

"I didn't look at his nose," interrupted Rhun excitedly. "But he called out: '*Ad adjuvandum me festina*.' No serf would shout for help in Latin."

"It's just what Eadgar would do, though," cried Osmund. "Which way did they go? Perhaps we can overtake them."

He rose, but Rhun pulled him down again.

"'Twere better the Harper should ask the Prince. See, he has sent Gwyllim Sassenach to invite him to play."

Osmund watched in a fever of impatience while Robin Hood strode up to the dais, saluted the company, and, sitting down, stretched out his strong, brown hand to the harp-strings.

"Will you not come up among us, friend?" said the Prince.

The knights and ladies courteously made room and Robin sprang lightly upon the dais, and in his jolly, ringing tones began to sing the ballad of *The Nut-Brown Maid*, strumming an accompaniment with rather more force than art.

After a moment Llewelyn laughed and laid a hand on the player's wrist.

"I think, friend, thy fingers are more accustomed to twang a bow-string than touch a harp," he cried. "Speak truth! Whose man art thou, and what doth an archer disguised as a minstrel?"

His young face became suddenly stern, and Osmund found himself trembling for his friend's safety.

"My lord, we came to beseech your help," he called, and pushed his way forward to Robin Hood's side.

The forester was no whit abashed.

"I am an archer first and foremost, as you truly guessed," he replied coolly. "But my business is with fleeing deer rather than armies. I am no man of war, but I can spin a quarter-staff, if need arise, and wrestle withal."

"I have no doubt thou canst," replied the Prince. "But speak to the point—tell me thy business and what brings thee into my country?"

"I came in pursuit of slavers who have carried off two children—the brother and sister of this lad here, and the boy a royal page to boot. We fear they are being taken through your dominions to Ireland, and are come to beg your aid."

Llewelyn turned to Gwyllim and asked a question and Rhun said something vehemently in Welsh. Two or three young men in the hall started up and, seizing their weapons, came forward, but the Prince shook his head.

"I am telling them we want peace, not war," he declared impatiently. "When will these hot-heads understand that everything cannot be settled by the sword! My grandfather Owen struggled with them for fifty years."

"Nevertheless, thy own sword has not slept in the scabbard!" exclaimed Gwyllim.

Llewelyn's eyes shone with a sudden angry light.

"Our swords and bright spears shall keep our country's boundaries," he said. "But are not to be used to slay our own kin. I have sent a youth to the courts of all the chieftains of Powys and Meirionydd: they must needs come here to do homage and pay the customary dues. Also we will send word that our ports shall be watched."

"But the men with whom these slavers deal will not use the King's ports like honourable sailors," said Robin bluntly. "There's many a lonely bit of coast-line where they can ship a cargo. Why, I have often—" He paused as he caught the young Prince's glance.

"It is the utmost I can promise at the present time," Llewelyn declared. "But tomorrow, when the chiefs arrive, I hope we may find means to allay your anxiety."

He then took leave of the company in a few courteous words, recommended the Saxon guests to the care of Gwyllim and Rhun, and withdrew to his private apartment.

While they had been on the dais the hall had been prepared for the night. Slaves had scattered fresh rushes and had carried in pillows and blankets to be distributed all along the wide sleeping-bench which lined the walls. The fire was carefully built up, and three young men sat down near it, wrapped in cloaks. It was their duty to tend it by turns all night.

Osmund took the first opportunity to repeat Rhun's information to Robin, but he was so dead-tired that he could not keep awake to talk things over as he had intended. As they lay down, the most heavenly strains of music sounded softly from the inner room. Never had either of them heard the harp touched by such a mighty hand.

"By my soul, I'll never call myself a harpist more!" exclaimed Robin softly as the sound died away. "Gwyllim, who plays? 'Tis never the same man who entertained us after supper!"

"'Tis the Prince himself," returned Gwyllim. "Young as he is there is no musician to touch him. And if you saw him leading his men in the field you would say the like—he has no peer."

CHAPTER TEN

"WAKE UP, WAKE UP! It is broad day and your master is abroad this hour!"

"What—where?" muttered Osmund. He opened his heavy eyes and saw a long ray of amber light striking the smoke-blackened beams of the roof far above him. For an instant he was quite bewildered and stared and blinked at Rhun, who was kneeling beside him.

"Are they found?" he cried at last, sitting up and throwing off the coverings.

"Not yet, I fear. But we thought perhaps you would like to come and see the place where Gwen and I saw them—at least if it was them."

"Yes. Wait a moment till I say my prayer," cried Osmund, jumping up. "And then we must find Master Robin."

"The men are all gone out to the horses," said Rhun. "But do you come with me—we can be back in twenty minutes, and by that time the cows will be milked and the folk will be serving out food and drink in the hall."

Osmund tightened his garters, slipped on his shoes and followed his new friend.

The hall was empty, but outside men and women were hard at work. Gwenllian was waiting for them on her pony, which she rode astride.

"Eluned won't come," she remarked. "Ever since little Sir Elian addressed an ode to her she thinks she is a beauty, and gives herself airs, and he only did it because he thought it would

71

please Llewelyn."

She led the way down the hillside, through a steep birch-wood: a river gleamed below, winding between lush meadows.

"We'll have to cross by the ford," said Rhun. "What a bother it must be to wear hosen! But you can ride the pony. I'll bring him back to you after Gwen has crossed."

"No, I thank you. It's easy to manage unless the water is very deep."

So saying Osmund kicked off his shoes, dragged up his chausses over the knee, and tied them to his belt with the strings provided for the purpose. He was glad to be wearing Much's peasant clothes instead of his own.

The sparkling water was quite warm though it was so early. The river was low and the rocks over which it flowed had been heated by the long hours of sunshine on the previous day. The three young people climbed up the opposite bank and followed the valley a little way until they came to a stream, spanned by an ancient, crumbling bridge.

"The country folk say the Romans built that," said Rhun. "Now here we climb up on the right of the stream, keeping to the edge of the great beech-wood."

"Peasants will not come here at night," remarked Gwenllian. "At least they won't go higher than the farm yonder. There are some strange heathen stones at the top, and it mightn't be lucky to meddle with them. But I'm not afraid," she added, and striking the pony with the green hazel-switch she held in her hand, she sent it scampering and scrambling up the hillside.

The boys ran after her, but soon slowed their pace to a walk. Osmund wanted to ask about Elian, and Rhun said he believed the little man hoped to be Llewelyn's family bard, but he did not think that the Prince would grant the appointment.

"Why," he added, "Gwen has gone right on to the head of the cwm! But this is the place where we saw the party. We were nutting, you see—though of course the hazels are not ripe yet. They were resting in this clump of hazels."

Osmund pushed aside the long, mottled rods and peered into the little clearing—then he made an exclamation and rushed forward. Something had caught his eyes, fixed into the fork of a bush. It was a long strip of gold-embroidered silk.

"Hild's girdle!" he exclaimed. "They have been here. Rhun, be careful—don't trample the ground—let's see which way the track goes."

"Why, that is plain enough. There were seven or eight horses, so it won't be difficult to follow them——"

"Seven or eight!" interrupted Osmund. "Look, there are the tracks of two or three score at least—the turf is cut up and trampled half a furlong wide."

"It may be the track of one of the chiefs riding down with his men to do fealty," suggested Rhun. "We had better find Gwen and go back at once to tell the Prince. See here—the traces of a group of horsemen mingles with the big troop—or maybe they have just followed the broad track."

He called his sister's name: "Gwenth—lian! Gwen!" but there was no answer.

"How far would she go? Is that the top of the hill?" asked Osmund, as they plodded up the steep path and noted that though the hoof-marks went in the same direction they kept to a little distance from the bridle-track.

"It is a couple of miles to the top," answered Rhun. "I expect she has only gone as far as the standing stones to prove she is not afraid of bogies."

"Let's run," said Osmund.

They hurried on and came out on a wind-blown grass-land which sloped upward to the horizon. Osmund noticed a raised green track in the turf, but before he had time to comment on it

Rhun pointed to a mound which rose out of the hillside against the sky.

"There, can you see the stones?" he was beginning when Gwen and her pony shot out from behind the hillock and galloped towards them. The pony plunged and struggled through the heather bushes and arrived with heaving flanks and lathered chest. Gwen too, looked scared.

"Let's get home, quick!" she cried.

"Did you see anything of the slavers?" asked Osmund as he and Rhun ran panting on either side of the pony.

"No—I saw nobody—I mean—oh, do let us get home!"

Gwen burst into tears, and then pretended that she was only coughing.

Rhun began to gasp out remarks in Welsh, and Osmund tried to tell of the finding of the girdle in English, but the girl seemed too much frightened and bewildered to take in what they were saying.

At last, half-way down the lane, Rhun laid his hand on the bridle and halted the pony.

"No one is following us, sister," he declared. "You know I have hearing as keen as a mountain roe's, and there is no step of man or steed in our wake."

Gwenllian shuddered and turned paler than ever.

"I fear not those whose footfall makes an echo," she whispered.

"What did you see?" demanded Osmund. "Witches, or fairies, or what?"

"God keep us from all harm!" exclaimed Gwen in Welsh. Then she added in English: "I will not tell you what I have seen, lest if there be evil it fall on you as well as me."

"Mother says ill-wishes can't hurt good Christians," declared Osmund cheerfully. "So tell *me*, maiden, if you fear to tell your brother."

He tried to speak consolingly, but Gwenllian jumped to the conclusion that he did not believe she had seen anything alarming at all, and she was greatly offended.

"Very well, Sassenach, be it as you wish!" she cried haughtily, and pushing Rhun violently aside she leant down and whispered in Osmund's ear. "The pony shied at something bright, and I jumped down and looked into a crack between the rocks. And I saw Arthur and all his Court!"

Osmund stared at her open-mouthed for a moment, then he grew angry in his turn.

"I see you are only playing!" he cried. "You do not understand that my sister's and brother's safety is more to me than life! I thought you had been frightened by robbers, and you begin a childish tale about Arthur, who has been dead five hundred years."

"But I saw them," protested Gwen. "How could I be deceived in broad daylight? And those who see Arthur before his time to return as King pine away and die."

"Anybody might pine away, if they neglect to break their fast!" exclaimed a cheerful voice, and Osmund shouted "Robin!" with great joy and relief.

The forester was sitting on the bank only a yard or two away, but hidden from the children by a holly bush. He got up in one swift, graceful movement and stepped forward.

"The maid is afraid," he said quickly. "Her hands are as cold as icicles. You are safe with me, child, I will not let any danger nigh you."

Gwen sobbed uncomforted.

"She thinks she has seen something unreal," said Rhun.

"Face a fear and it is halved," said Robin. "March boldly upon it and 'twill melt away. I fear nobody, for no good man has cause of grief against me."

"She says she saw Arthur and all his Court," remarked Osmund.

"Oh," returned Robin thoughtfully. "That were a wondrous sight, *pardi*! And did they bear bows like me, maiden, or were they unarmed?"

"They were all in greaves and breastplates," answered Gwen. "And their helms lay beside them, and a spear was at each man's knee."

"Oh," said Robin again. He turned his head and glanced steadily up the mountain behind them. He watched the trees and bushes and the movements of the wild birds, all intent on their own business; then he listened. They all listened, but there was no sound but the sweet, inconclusive babble of the stream.

"Master Robin, look—we found this," cried Osmund, showing the girdle. "It is Hild's—I am sure of it."

Robin nodded but did not answer. He began to lead the pony forward, while Osmund went on eagerly talking. When the bridge came in sight, Robin stopped.

"Listen," he said solemnly. "Can you keep counsel? Will you, Rhun, take your sister home and tell this strange tale to none until I rejoin you?"

"Fair sir, you are a stranger," said the Welsh boy bluntly. "Is it not against my duty to hide anything from my patron, the Prince?"

"Tell him in private then," agreed Robin, "and add this word: When the wind is in the heather, but the tree is still, let the Chief gather his friends, and the deer sleep on the hill."

"We'll go swiftly," cried Rhun. "Youth," he added, turning to Osmund, "jump up behind Gwen: I'll run."

"Nay, I'll stay with Robin Hood," declared Osmund.

Rhun wasted no more words but scrambled on to the pony and started it towards the river at a gallop.

Osmund whirled round, prepared to run straight up the hillside again, but Robin stood quite still, his feet apart, his brown, curly head thrown back, absorbed in gazing first in one direction then in another. At last he began to walk slowly upstream.

"Passing strange," he muttered. "Perhaps the little lass was inventing after all. Or could she have been right? If there was aught human astir up there the birds would give us tidings."

"Could there be anything *not* human?" inquired Osmund, with a most unpleasant, creepy feeling running up and down his spine.

"We'll soon see," said Robin. "But if you would rather follow your friends, or wait me here, I'll think no worse of you—for joking apart, I have no idea at all what might be on the hilltop."

"Whatever it is, I'm coming with you," said Osmund. "Why, Robin, surely you don't think I would run away if you are going into danger?"

"Come you from courage or curiosity?" inquired Robin, who did not believe in taking anything over seriously.

"Curiosity, of course!"

Before the words were out of Osmund's mouth, Robin had leaped the stream, landing with unerring balance on a slippery stone, and was gliding through the tangle of young wood on the farther side as quickly and noiselessly as a questing hound. He paused from time to time to peer up at the horizon, and at one of these pauses pointed out the gulls circling lazily round and round in the warm summer air.

"There is carrion or offal of some kind there—mark the gulls! But a few moments ago plover flew steadily over, so there can scarce be men about."

"It might be just a dead sheep," hazarded the boy.

"Would there be sheep up there exposed to wolves and foxes without a shepherd? But of course shepherds may have left a dead beast unburied."

They went on; presently the stream bent to the left, and Robin crossed back. Osmund pointed out the hazel grove, and when they came to the traces of horses Robin whistled under his breath. He did not stop to examine either track but hastened on till they reached the edge of the beechwood and faced the wide sweep of heathery hill.

"Oh, look, Robin!" cried Osmund. "There's a road! A secret road—I mean a Roman road, like the one at home."

He pointed to the grassy causeway raised above the level of the moor.

Robin made no answer. He was sniffing the breeze. Above them the queer circle of stones crowned the little hill and jutted out against the sky.

"What said the maid?" he whispered.

"Why—she said she rode round the camp—as she called it— and something glittered in the sun, and she got off the pony to look, and through a crack between two rocks she saw a company of armed men and——"

"That's all I want to know," interrupted Robin. "See, here went the pony's feet, crushing the turf. And here we must follow; stay to my right and don't speak a word."

Robin strode on, keeping his own body between Osmund and the point whence danger threatened—the largest jutting stone which might well hide a man.

CHAPTER ELEVEN

WONDERFUL TALES were current of the strange persons and creatures that might be met with in Wales. Robin Hood was none too sure of his ground: even highly educated people believed in monsters and fairies, and he was quite prepared to believe that a poetical Welsh child might see a vision of her country's hero. On the other hand he was shrewd and had no intention of being slain in someone else's quarrel—hence he circled the mound at a good bowshot from the stones. Having satisfied himself that there was no movement about them, he dropped down behind the slight shelter of the raised track and crawled cautiously forward until he was able to creep between the tall heather bushes which covered the base of the hillock. Osmund copied him as faithfully as he could, but was soon gasping for breath and streaming with perspiration as he worked his way along.

From time to time Robin raised his head with infinite precaution and scanned the hill-side: some feeding curlew had risen and were flying about aloft in a way which would certainly have given them away had there been anyone watching—they would drop down as though to alight and then sweep upward again with frightened cries.

At last, after a long halt, Robin writhed his long form into a winding sheep-track and advanced boldly up the mount. The dewy path bore the impress of the pony's little feet and rose steeply to within a few yards of the standing stones. Sundry huge fragments of rock, which had once perhaps formed part of the circle, lay where they had fallen centuries before, and Robin examined each in turn. As he parted the rough grass and seedling whins, which sprouted about the third crag, he gave a smothered exclamation and recoiled violently on top of Osmund.

"Lord protect us!" muttered Robin. "Keep back, lad, I reckon it's no canny sight."

Osmund made the Sign of the Cross very carefully.

"Where you look, I look," he said, and creeping forward he craned his head over a dark fissure between two great slabs of stone. For a moment he could see nothing save a little fern bleached by the darkness, which fluttered in the draught from below. Then something glittered and the amazing scene became visible, like something painted on a dark background. He was looking into a cavern where men in armour were lying one on top of another—dead, as he thought at first. Then as he stared he became aware of red faces and open mouths from which came noisy breaths.

"Robin—they are drunken men!" he whispered. "They are real—no phantasy."

But though he spoke boldly his shaking limbs would scarcely hold him up. Creeping a little nearer, Osmund thrust his head into the cleft; at the same moment Robin approached and pressed down a large frond of bracken, letting a ray of light stream into the cave.

"Why," muttered Osmund, "we're dreaming! There lies Sir Elian, or his double."

Robin Hood pushed him aside and stared down for a tense minute. There was Sir Elian sure enough, gagged and bound like a criminal, and as Robin gazed he saw two small hands, tied together, stretch out from the darkness and shake the little man urgently by the arm.

Osmund was startled to hear Robin Hood whisper:

"We be friends. Lie still and make no sound."

Then he squatted back on his heels and laughed soundlessly.

"Blackbird, Blackbird! I wager we have all our quarry under our feet. But 'tis a ticklish pass, and drunken men—if they wake—are ill to reckon with. I'll wage a hart royal to a coney but we'll find Eadgar and the lass here as well."

He crept into the circle; it was a wide, grassy space with a large, flat stone in the centre; it would not budge under his hand and seemed firmly bedded in the earth. The grass was trampled and there were remains of food flung about as though a large body of men had bivouacked there.

"Ha," muttered Robin, "the gulls hinted as much."

There was no sign of horses. Looking back along the way they had come, Robin decided that the horses must be hidden somewhere in the beechwood. He scrambled down the farther side of the mound, taking care not to show himself on the skyline, and presently discovered a hole under a large rock—such a hole as a fox might make only that a strong draught blew from it. Robin tested the rock with his hand and it rolled slightly; then he put forth all his strength, but could not budge it further.

"It is wedged on the inner side," he declared.

"I could get under it," whispered Osmund. "If we scrape away these small stones and gravel, I could wriggle through."

"We'll try the other rock first," declared the forester, and he went back to the original place, while Osmund scraped and tore at the turf until his hands were bleeding. When Robin Hood returned after vainly seeking for another entrance, Osmund had disappeared all but his feet which he now drew after him with a last convulsive movement.

It was a horrible moment as he pushed himself forward under the rock, his hands grasping slimy clay, his chin scraping on the soil. At length he was able to kneel up, and he found himself in a rude passage, where there was only room to advance on all fours. He felt for his knife and crept forward with it in his hand. His stealthy movements seemed to make a great deal of noise, his breathing alone filled his ears. But presently loud snores from the cavern drowned every other sound, and creeping through the low entrance Osmund found himself in a large circular chamber. There was a strong smell of mead, and as his eyes became accustomed to the dim light he could see a huge cauldron in the centre of the cave, and horns still clasped in the sleepers' hands. His heart beat hard as he cautiously picked his way through the men. There were two or three persons of high degree among the soldiers, for they wore gold collars, hooked round their throats by twisted gold wire, just like Llewelyn and his kinsfolk.

A sniffing sound made the boy start violently. It came again—sniff, sniff! There was a second smaller cave opening out of the big one, and as he gazed towards it, clutching his dagger, a ruffled, dark head was raised from the floor, and Eadgar's eyes met his.

Osmund flattened himself against the wall—it was made of beaten clay—and crept slowly and carefully towards his brother. Eadgar's arms were tied behind him: his feet too were fastened together and he was gagged. It was very difficult to release him in the darkness: Osmund was afraid of hurting him, and was slow and bungling over the work. Together they found Hild and released her too, and Osmund hugged her silently. But when he stooped over Sir Elian Hild pinched him.

"He has had a lot of mead," she whispered.

Elian's eyes rolled despairingly, and Osmund wavered.

"He tried to rescue us—we can't leave him," declared Eadgar.

"Leave his gag then," said Hild.

Osmund cut the thongs which bound the little man's hands and put his dagger into them.

"Free your feet and follow me," he said, and while Elian was rubbing his numb fingers and fumbling with the dagger,

Osmund led the way past the snoring drunkards and pushed Hild before him down the passage. She stooped down and wriggled under the stone like a flash. The boys paused an instant to see if they could discover the mechanism by which the great slab was poised, but a noise behind them made them abandon the attempt. Robin's hand could be seen wildly groping under the stone and closing and unclosing in his frenzied impatience, so first one boy and then the other crept out on the hillside. The noise they had heard proved to have been caused by Sir Elian, who tripped over a steel helmet and sent it rolling with a clatter. No one was more frightened than himself, and Robin laughed so much as Elian's pale, agitated face appeared—still tightly gagged—that he could hardly exert his strength to drag him out.

"No time to lose," he said then, and caught up Hild in his arms. "Lads, take the dwarf one on each side. Come, Elian, run for the honour of Wales and the safety of Llewelyn!"

He leaped down the hillside as he spoke, swerving towards the beechwood. The boys followed, dragging Elian with them.

Far away on the opposite hill they heard the silver music of a bugle, and at the gallant sound a horse neighed below them in the coppice.

Robin stopped suddenly and looked back.

"There should be just time to break up their horse-lines," he cried. "Oh, Elian, what a tale this will make when thou canst open thy lips to tell it!"

He dived into the wood and the others, panting in his wake, came presently to lines of picketed horses. There seemed to be no one on guard, and still clutching Hild against his shoulder, Robin rushed down the rows, kicking the pegs out of the ground and slashing at the ropes with his knife. Soon a score of excited animals were plunging about, and the boys, by Robin's command, bridled four stout cobs and they all mounted.

FIRST ONE BOY AND THEN THE OTHER CREPT OUT ON THE HILLSIDE

"No time for saddles!" cried Robin, and picking a long sapling he drove the loose horses before him, and sent them galloping wildly down the lane towards the river.

"If the folk up yonder are truly coming to do homage to the Prince of Aberffraw, they will not be best pleased with us," remarked Robin with a grin. "Elian may be some private enemy of theirs for all we know——"

"Nay, Robin," interrupted Eadgar, "the little man came to our aid and they threatened to slay him and then decided to keep him as a hostage. He said they are traitors and intend to surround Llewelyn's camp and put him to death."

"Good, strong beer seems to have interfered with their plans," remarked the forester. "Now, children, cross the ford: I will wait till you are safe over for fear of accidents. Ride close, Blackbird, and I'll put this little maid behind you."

"It wasn't beer it was mead," announced a dismal, croaking voice.

Elian had at last managed to work off the gag, which still hung round his neck. He intended to take up his position opposite Robin Hood in order to share his post as guard of the ford, but his pony decided otherwise and trotted nimbly in the wake of the others, with its rider clinging to its mane.

"Are not you coming, Master Robin?" called the children from the opposite bank.

"Nay—bid the Prince send a few archers to hold the ford——"

Before the words were out of his mouth a group of horsemen came galloping down from the Hall. The foremost wore a mantle of scarlet silk and a helmet surmounted by a scarlet wolf's head. It was Llewelyn himself.

While the Prince paused to speak to Elian, Robin dismounted, tied up his pony and produced the bow and quiver which he had previously hidden in the rushes at the water's brink. He selected an arrow with his customary coolness and glanced keenly at the thicket from which the enemy might be expected to emerge.

"Two hundred paces," he muttered. "'Twere best to aim at the track where it turns above the bridge."

"Let us over-run the woods like the wolf," exclaimed Gwyllim, speaking English for Robin's benefit. "Let their blood crimson the tide of the stream."

"Gently," said Llewelyn. "Their swords are still in the scabbard. We have but one man's testimony against them."

"They enlisted the slavers to fight for them," cried Elian, his voice cracking with rage. And he began to pour forth poetic vituperations which left Gwyllim's remarks completely in the shade.

"Let no man strike till I give the word," ordered Llewelyn; he glanced sternly round to see if his warriors were prepared to obey him. "Will you ride with us, Master Archer? We will encircle the hill and take them in the rear, while my two kinsmen here and their men keep the ford."

"I have not my harp," cried Elian, "but nevertheless I will sing the song of the onset."

"But first," said Llewelyn kindly, "you must have your wounds dressed and take some refreshment. You, fair children, lead him to the Hall and stay you all within the enclosure until we return. Do you understand? It is my command."

"Do as he says," shouted Robin, above the rippling water.

"We will obey," said Eadgar, speaking for them all.

Osmund heaved a deep sigh. He greatly longed to ride beside Robin and to see the end of the adventure. Llewelyn turned to him.

"You shall be my representative," he said. "Take this as a token to the Lady Cristin, my kinswoman, and she will provide entertainment for you all."

He laid a beautiful rosary of chased gold in Osmund's hand and went forward across the river.

CHAPTER TWELVE

THE LADIES of Llewelyn's family were standing at the entrance of the courtyard, gazing anxiously in the wake of the horsemen.

Osmund felt very awkward as he slipped down from his pony and came forward with Llewelyn's rosary in his hand. All the womenfolk, the serfs and the old Seneschal burst into Welsh speech, sounding for all the world like a flock of starlings settling for the night in the great holly tree beyond the moat at home.

Luckily Rhun was there and he translated Osmund's shy speeches, and all the ladies then clustered round Elian and Hild and Eadgar, with even shriller outcry.

It must be owned that Hild immensely enjoyed the sensation she had created and longed to be able to relate her experiences. The two brothers stole away to a quiet corner, where Gwen presently followed them with a foaming mug of new milk in one hand and a large dish of oaten flummery in the other. There were two spoons, one of gold and the other of horn, and the boys fell to with a will, sharing the bowl between them. They talked hard between mouthfuls.

Presently Rhun joined them, carrying a big platter of bilberries and cream and a pile of buttered oat-cake.

"The ladies are all ministering to the bard," he said. "They hope he will put their names in his next ode and say that they are all divinely beautiful."

"There seem to be a great many bards in Wales," said Eadgar.

"I wish I could understand Welsh—I know they have wonderful rules for their verse—it must be very interesting."

"My father was a poet," said Rhun. "But he died before I can remember. His name was Howel, and after his death we were sent as hostages to Randulf Blundeville at Chester."

"So that is where you learnt English," said Osmund.

"Yes, and French too. He is married to the Lady Constance, you know, the heiress of Brittany, and the Bretons are kin to the Cymri. Only for her and her son Arthur, Randulf would have killed us both. Why do the English kill hostages? I think it is most unjust."

"I suppose it is when a treaty is broken or something," said Eadgar. "When barons begin warring with each other, they don't seem to mind a bit whom they kill. Except knights like my father, of course—true and faithful knights."

"Like Llewelyn too," agreed Rhun.

"I think Prince Llewelyn is splendid," cried Osmund warmly. "I should think his knights would follow him everywhere like Arthur's. I say, isn't it rather a joke that Gwen's Knights of the Round Table prove to be a crew of drunken enemies?"

They all burst into shouts of laughter.

"All the same, who could tell what was there?" cried Eadgar, interrupting himself. "My father will be proud of Osmund when I tell him the tale."

"That was nothing—Robin Hood was with me!" exclaimed Osmund, flushing at his brother's praise.

"Not when you crept under that rock," declared Eadgar. "I shall put it all in my chronicle. Hild was very brave too."

"Let's see if there is any sign of the men," cried Osmund, to change the subject, and they all went to the door.

The gate of the enclosure was barred, but by climbing an ash tree they were able to look over it. There was nothing to be seen except peasants peacefully cutting hay, and swans sailing on the river, and great shining white clouds rising slowly behind Llantisilio Mountain. But far away Osmund detected the gay lilt of a horn.

Tantivy-tantivy-tan-tallo!

"That's Robin Hood!" he cried. "It's the home call and means that all goes well."

An hour later the warriors returned. They had vanquished the rebels after a sharp skirmish and had taken their leader. Meredith ap Conan, prisoner. Two of the slavers had been killed in the fight, the others had fled. Robin Hood had done gallant service and was unhurt. As soon as he could push his way through the throng he called the boys and asked if they had done anything about Elian's harp. Osmund was obliged to confess that he had never once remembered it, but Gwen, who was standing by, declared that her sister had put it safely aside. Robin sent Osmund to the river for silver sand, and Eadgar to whisper in Elian's ear that his harp was found and would be restored to him by supper-time.

"We cannot, in courtesy, depart today," said Robin. "Though maybe Elian will find us a messenger by whom we can get word to Little-John that he may send back the Castle men with the tidings that you are safe."

"Make him find the messenger before you give him the harp," suggested Osmund, laughing.

Robin thought this a good suggestion, and while he was talking the matter over with the little bard, Gwyllim Sassenach came up and very civilly proposed to take the message himself.

"For that kindness, we must offer him the least good of our two Spanish horses," said Robin, as he and the boys sat on the grass scrubbing most unmercifully at the frame of the harp.

"And how shall we get gold to repay the beggar?" inquired Osmund. "Had we not better send a letter to our mother, asking her to provide it as soon as she can?"

"Nay, there is no haste. The beggar can stay in my band and

I will settle the matter with him in due time. When you go adventuring with me, Blackbird, Heaven provides the cost."

"But, Robin, you came for our sake," cried Eadgar. "And never can we repay you for saving us from worse than death. I do not know how to thank you, Master Robin, but if ever you have a service a boy can do, I'll be proud to render it."

"And I too!" exclaimed Osmund.

Hilda had been carried off by the Welsh girls to their own inner room. She appeared at the feast that evening, beautifully dressed in one of Gwen's garments, with a gold collar round her neck, and a green fillet in her hair.

Llewelyn noticed her and said she looked more like a dryad than a maid, and no one there, except his chaplain, a learned monk from the new Abbey of Valle Crucis, had the least idea what he meant. Rhun and his sisters were allowed to sit with the visitors, and they pointed out the notables who had come to the feast. All day the neighbouring lords had been riding in to do homage, and now, towards evening, folk from further away came hurrying up, for the news of the skirmish had spread like wild-fire. The fierce tribesmen of Meirionydd were eager to protest their loyalty, and the more sophisticated chieftains from Maelor and the border were not to be outdone.

Rhun pointed out Ednyved Vychan, a chief of Gwynedd, who was Llewelyn's great friend; his wife, Gwenllian was godmother to Rhun's sister.

"And the lady in white velvet is Eva, the daughter of Madoc-ap-Meredith—she's supposed to be wonderfully beautiful—white as the spray on the wave and all that."

The boys glanced critically at the young woman in question.

"She is very fair but I like Maid Marian's looks better," remarked Osmund. "Maid Marian would look beautiful whatever she wore—she has such laughing eyes."

"Her voice makes you glad," chimed in Eadgar.

"I could not praise her better myself," said Robin, "and I would she were here."

The Welsh drank from horns, and Robin Hood had been supplied with a large one, mounted in gold, and filled to the brim with wine. He rose to his feet and trolled forth:

> "I drink to the maid
> Of the forest glade
> And fair she is to see,
> Her eyes are bright
> As the stars o' night,
> And her shape like the sapling tree.

> "In weal or woe
> She will with me go,
> For truer than gold is she,
> By my arrow and bow
> I can prove it so,
> O, the archer's target is she."

With the last words he emptied his horn in one prolonged draught.

"Well sung, Master Archer," exclaimed Llewelyn. "There is a pretty play upon words in the last line, for I warrant the lady is the target of your thoughts and her prayers your shield in danger."

Robin bowed civilly: plays upon words were more than he could manage, though he could throw off a rhyme easily enough.

"If you had consulted me, my good friend, I would have polished the rude verse for you," said Elian patronizingly. "Why, even for the English mode you should have alliteration, if not assonance."

"Heavens!" muttered Robin. "I'd rather have eel-pie," and he helped himself generously to the said dainty. "Here, Eadgar, change places with me—alliterance and assonation are more in your line than mine."

Eadgar obeyed, and soon he and the bard were deep in discussion, passing from the rules of poetry to the quotation of syllogisms. It was observed that Eadgar forgot his food in his absorption, but that Elian never missed a dish, though he talked without ceasing.

He was called upon presently for a song, and came forward with great dignity, bearing his recovered harp—somewhat scratched as to frame, but none the worse otherwise. He had an ode all ready and introduced a special verse to praise Robin Hood. Otherwise the ode, though ostensibly in honour of Llewelyn, was all about the prowess of Elian, who seemed to think that he had waylaid the rebel Meredith and captured him single-handed.

The children were sitting round the hearth by this time, and Rhun whispered this comment. Mischievous Hild pulled a charred stick from the fire and drew on the clean flagstone a lively caricature of the little man, crawling from under the rock. Eadgar rubbed it out with his foot, but not before Rhun and Gwenllian had hailed it with appreciative giggles.

When Elian had finished his ode he struck up a livelier air and began to sing 'englynion'—a particular kind of extempore verse, with sly jokes against some person or persons in the audience. Soon the lords and ladies at the upper end of the hall began to stand up in turns and sing each an englyn in reply—then the folk at the lower end had their chance.

The English children could not understand the words, but they laughed when the other people laughed, and enjoyed watching the people jump up and take part. Eluned said the fun would be kept up till one or two in the morning. It was a regular 'Merry Night' she said, such as they often had in Wales. People would gather from all the houses and farms about and each one would bring something to eat or drink, so as to make things easy for the host and hostess.

When it grew late the Lady Cristin sent the girls to bed in one of the inner rooms. The boys rolled themselves up in the coarse, home-made blankets which were spread over heaps of sweet-smelling rushes on the sleeping-bench. The noise of laughter, singing and playing went on as merrily as ever, and whenever they opened their eyes the great fire was flaming vigorously and no one seemed to dream of breaking up the party.

.   .   .   .   .

The 'merry night' fun was indeed kept up until light began to dawn. At last the harps were wheeled aside, blankets were spread and the ladies withdrew. Llewelyn invited Robin Hood to walk out with him into the fresh air. Such guests as could not be accommodated in the hall were making their way to tents and huts set up within the enclosure. Llewelyn bade the porter open the outer doors and strode up the pasture to the hill-top, where he paused and looked around him.

"See, friend," he said. "Those little white buildings scattered like stars on the green are churches. Mass will be said anon all over this land of ours, and we are Christian men."

"Yet your cousin could plot treachery against you and find a following too," remarked Robin. His keen eyes wandered from one simple little barn-like building to another: from the eminence on which they stood four or five were to be seen. They were whitewashed all over, including the reed-thatched roofs.

"The Prince of Peace dwells in our midst," said the Welshman. "And for His sake, and for my policy of peace, I will not slay Meredith. Nevertheless, I must keep him prisoned until my power is supreme."

"And then you will attack England, I suppose?" said Robin cheerfully.

"Not unless your King attacks me. I would even do homage to Richard, if he would keep his barons in order. 'Tis my mind that the two countries should be as sisters, the older protecting the younger. Yes, England should guard the Eastern confines of the land and repel invaders. We can keep our coasts ourselves."

"You will pardon me, Sir Prince, but are you not very young to direct a princedom single-handed? But no doubt you have councillors?" said Robin, stifling a yawn.

"My father, Davydd, was my counsellor," said Llewelyn. "He impressed his views on my mind when I was a child. 'Strike with the sword only as a last extremity,' he taught me, 'and then strike hard.'"

"Good counsel," agreed Robin. "Would it be deemed a discourtesy if I slept awhile beneath that group of rowan trees? For I am not used to lying under a roof."

"It were safer within the garth. But, good fellow, I brought you here to ask you—will you not throw in your lot with ours for a while? My cousins would like marvellous well to have your young friends for playmates."

"Aye, but the Lady Etheldreda expects me to bring them back without delay," cried Robin.

"Then when my affairs are more settled, you, good Sir Forester, must visit us at my own castle at Aber," said Llewelyn kindly.

"With all my heart!" Robin rejoined.

The young Prince held out his hand with that gracious friendliness which won all hearts to him. After the hand-clasp, he took a silk purse from under his mantle; the long ends hung down, heavily weighted, and the gleam of gold showed through the strands.

"I would not have you the poorer for your sojourn in Wales," he said, and laid his gift on Robin's palm.

"Great thanks," cried the forester, carelessly sticking the purse in his belt. "A good gift, nobly bestowed! And may I, in my turn, crave your acceptance of my Spanish horse? The other I would fain give to Gwyllim in gratitude for his kindness."

Llewelyn could not forbear a smile at the way in which Robin Hood linked prince and vassal in his bestowal of 'vails' or parting gifts. He was accustomed to be treated with almost exaggerated consideration in his own court, and his ancient lineage and exalted position were always being brought forward.

But it was evident that Robin spoke in all simplicity, and with no intention of giving offence.

"It is a noble gift, and Gwyllim and I thank you most heartily," cried Llewelyn. "When I ride in the jousts, or to meet your King—in conference—I will bestride your horse."

"Good day, then," said the forester.

He did not wait to be dismissed by the Prince, but turned aside to the cluster of mountain ash trees and rolling himself in his cloak, threw himself down to rest.

Presently a little bell, hung over the roof of a white-washed chapel in the valley, began to ring the Angelus.

Robin Hood got up and said the prayer, for he was ever most devout to Our Blessed Lady.

He noted that Llewelyn too was praying, still standing at his vantage-point on the hilltop, with his tall figure silhouetted against the sunrise.

Robin Hood only slept for a couple of hours and then strolled down to the hall to break his fast. Sentries had been posted overnight, and he was not allowed to pass until Gwyllim came out, yawning, and brought him in. The children were up and had gone to see the cows milked. The Welsh attached great importance to their herds and milk, and its products formed a large portion of their diet.

"Some day you must come to visit us," said Gwen. "And you shall ride my pony, and we'll share everything with you. What fun it will be to show you our mountains."

"I'll take you fishing in the lakes," said Rhun.

"And I'll show you where the little yellow water-lilies grow," said Eluned. "We have a Roman road, too, which comes right down the mountain to our Castle—Llewelyn says there are Roman milestones on it, and we could go and look for them."

"Who told you about *our* Roman road?" asked Hild. "It's a secret and nobody is to know!"

"How can it be a secret?" exclaimed Rhun. "Everyone is aware that the Saxons did not know how to make roads—as we Cymri do—and all the highways you have in England are Roman ones."

Osmund glanced at his brother: it was surely the scholar of the family who ought to be able to refute a remark like that. But Eadgar was following out his own train of thought.

"I never told any secret," he said slowly. "I said we were tracing out an old Roman road when we walked into the slavers' camp unawares. I didn't say where we started from."

"English folk are as good road-builders as anyone else—better!" declared Osmund, as it seemed as though Eadgar would not take up the challenge. "But we have the sense to use the good Roman roads when they are there—some of them. And we make new roads too."

"But we are free as birds, or the wild deer that wander over the hill," said Rhun. "We scorn roads—our good little mountain horses carry us wherever we will."

"One Roman road always leads to another Roman road," remarked Eadgar, still tenacious of his idea. "And so at last they all lead to Rome, like the spokes of a wheel going to the same centre."

"I have an idea!" cried Osmund. "Perhaps *our* road leads to Rhun's road, and some day we'll all come riding down it to visit the Prince. You had better give us a password, so that your folk will know us when we come."

"It must be something about Arthur," chimed in Gwen eagerly. "Arthur's cave—Ogof Arthur—how would that do?"

Eadgar had been listening to the children without speaking, and now seeing Llewelyn's chaplain, Friar Gwryd, emerge from the house, he waylaid him.

"Is it not true, good Friar, that one Roman road leads to another?" he asked eagerly. "I know you are a learned man, and can give me a safe answer."

"Why, as to that, I am better read in spiritual matters than in worldly ones," returned the priest, smiling. "They say 'all roads lead to Rome,' so it was true once; but since the time of the Roman occupation of England many hundred years have flown. So, doubtless, rivers have changed their courses and roads have been ploughed up, interrupted or built upon."

"We still use Watling Street and Rycknield Street, and the Fosse Way as main highways," declared Eadgar.

"We have Sarn Helen connecting North and South Wales, and merchants occasionally use it," said Gwryd. "But this is deep talk for such an early hour, and I must leave you to say Mass in the church below there."

"Give us ten minutes to make our farewells, and we will hear your Mass," cried Robin Hood. "Quick, children, get your cloaks—give your thanks—we must be gone!"

Elian, roused by one of the serfs, came hurrying out to bid them farewell.

"You will find me when you visit the Prince," he declared. "For I am duly appointed Household Bard as a reward for my share in yesterday's noble slaughter."

"H'm, three men killed and a few wounded," commented Rhun in Osmund's ear.

Robin waved his cap and rode on down the slope, followed

helter-skelter by the children. Eluned walked behind with great sedateness until a turn in the path took her out of sight of the Hall, and then she ran faster than any of them.

The little church was very poor—there were no chairs or benches and everyone knelt on the floor. A circle of peasants were gathered round the altar, with their dogs crouching at their feet. The men joined in the responses to the Mass, and at the moment of the Elevation a great sigh went up from all: "Welcome to the Son of Mary!"

As soon as Mass was over Robin Hood went out and jumped on to his cob. He did not love prolonged farewells, and was anxious to rejoin his band. But before he could move off Rhun came hastening up.

"The Prince sends you this ring," he said, holding up a jewel set in delicate Celtic craftsmanship. "He says 'twill be your passport when you come to visit him. You have only to show it and say his name, and his vassals will bring you to him wherever he may be."

Robin thanked him, and pulling up a chain which hung about his neck, slung the ring on to it in company with a medal of Our Lady and one of St. Hubert, patron of hunters.

The journey to Southwell was uneventful. The Lady Etheldreda had received Robin's message some days previously, and was therefore out of acute anxiety. Stephen thought the time would never pass; he could not settle either to work or play, but was continually running from window to window to see if his brothers and sister were yet in sight.

Stephen and Sibell were saying their night prayers in the chapel when at last the lilt of Robin's bugle came to their ears. The Manor House was so near the Minster that the lady only had a small oratory in the battlements, with a slit in the wall through which a sentry could hear Mass without leaving his post. No sentries were posted during times of peace, so Sibell and her brother sprang up from their prayers and hurried out to the windy platform. Sibell was not tall enough to look over the parapet, and Stephen could not see anything in the gathering dusk. So they rushed down to tell their mother that Robin was coming, and then to carry her orders to the lieutenant to lift the portcullis and drop the drawbridge. After that, they had to wait for what seemed ages until the bugle sang again and the sound of trotting horses sounded first far away, then clattering on the village cobblestones, and at last, soft and dull, mounting up the grassy slope.

Stephen and Sibell rushed out and were the first to greet the wanderers. Robin Hood, Hild, and the boys rode at the head, followed by Scarlet, Friar Tuck, Little-John, Much, and many another old friend. The lady came running into the courtyard with her veil flying out behind her and seized her children in her arms.

All was bustle in the house. The cook sent the scullions to the poultry-yard to slay half-a-dozen fowl. He had the pie-crusts for huge pasties all ready in the buttery, and soon savoury smells streamed forth from the kitchen. Sam butler broached a new barrel of ale, Dame Alice insisted on embracing Eadgar, and all was a joyous hubbub.

Robin Hood and his followers departed at dawn next day, and the children of the Castle settled down to their usual work and play as though the exciting adventures of the past week had never happened.

The End

ALSO BY AGNES BLUNDELL

View a sample chapter from each title at www.staidanpress.com.

THE NET

"Roger felt a freezing dew break out upon his forehead. The net was over him it seemed; in vain he told himself that he could establish his identity. His head was worth forty pounds to the vile creatures at the stair foot, and once in their clutches who knew if he could ever communicate with his friends?"

$16.00 — 264 pages. Available at amazon.com.

THEY MET ROBIN HOOD

Osmund does a good turn to one of Robin Hood's outlaws and makes friends with the band. But how can outlaws help his family against a friend of Prince John?

$15.00 — 214 pages. Available at amazon.com.

OTHER TITLES AVAILABLE FROM ST. AIDAN PRESS

THE QUEEN'S TRAGEDY, by Msgr. Robert Hugh Benson

"Upon the publication of former books of mine several kindly critics remarked that the reign of Mary Tudor told a very different story with regard to the Catholic character. It is that story which I am now attempting to set forth as honestly as I can."

$19.00 — 364 pages. Available at amazon.com.

MANGLED HANDS, by Fr. Neil Boyton, S.J.

Tarcisius Tandihetsi, the chief's son, has seen wonderful things in the Great Villages of the French and is going home. But the canoes are ambushed by the Iroquois, and he will soon learn what it is to be a captive alone among pagans. If only he could escape and find his Blackrobe, Father Isaac Jogues!

$14.00 — 186 pages. Available at amazon.com.

REDROBES, by Fr. Neil Boyton, S.J.

Thirteen-year-old orphan Jacques gets into trouble in Quebec, and decides to run away to Huronia and become an interpreter for his

Jesuit guardian, Father John Brebeuf. But his journey along the Iroquois-infested river may not be so easy as he hopes!

$17.00 — 300 pages. Available at amazon.com.

THE ANCHORHOLD, by Enid Dinnis

A chaplain's sermon drove Editha de Beauville to give up the world and enter the religious life. But could a strong-willed noblewoman accept and embrace full seclusion in an anchorhold? Read on to learn how she fared, and how her life affected those around her: Sir Aleric, her erstwhile suitor, now a crusader knight; Fr. Nicholas, a young priest who was quite bright, and thought so too; and Fiddlemee, the witty yet wise court jester whose past held a surprising secret.

$14.00 — 196 pages. Available at amazon.com.

THE ROAD TO SOMEWHERE, by Enid Dinnis

Richard and Ann discover a real Tudor house in London being sold cheap, complete with leather latch-strings, a tale of hidden treasure, and a wonderful piper. But the treasure turns out to be an old altar-stone. Will it lose them the house and each other, or set them on the real road to Somewhere?

$10.00 — 106 pages. Available at amazon.com.

THE SHEPHERD OF WEEPINGWOLD, by Enid Dinnis

Sir Robert Luffkyn, rich grandson of a peasant, has purchased the manor of Weepingwold from the noble but impoverished de Lessels, intending to make the renamed Luffkynwold a busy center of his tanning trade. He sends Petronilla, last de Lessels, to Gracerood, intending her for its future Abbess, and plucks little Brother Kit from the cloister to become the new parson of the long-abandoned church. How will Father Kit fare with the parish and his own soul? Will Petronilla find her true vocation? And is there really a witch in the parish?

$14.00 — 202 pages. Available at amazon.com.

SCOUTING FOR SECRET SERVICE, by Fr. Bernard F. J. Dooley

Frank and George are going to spend their summer vacation in the Adirondacks, thanks to Frank's uncle Ed. But once they get there, they realize something fishy is going on. Can they trust Pete, their Indian guide, or is he mixed up in it too? And is Frank's mysterious uncle really behind it all?

$14.00 — 188 pages. Available at amazon.com.

THE COMING OF THE MONSTER, by Fr. Owen Francis Dudley

The Masterful Monk returns to England to fight against the Bolshevik cause, to find beautiful, idealistic Verna Wray torn between her family's wealth and her French Catholic suitor. But how much suffering is Red hate still to cause them all?

$15.00 — 218 pages. Available at amazon.com.

THE MASTERFUL MONK, by Fr. Owen Francis Dudley

Brother Anselm comes back to England to counter the Atheist's efforts to destroy the influence of Catholic morals. Between his lectures he is drawn into a struggle for the soul of Beauty Dethier, who is Catholic but fascinated by the "freedom" of the world and the Atheist.

$18.00 — 342 pages. Available at amazon.com.

WILL MEN BE LIKE GODS? & THE SHADOW ON THE EARTH, by Fr. Owen Francis Dudley

Father Dudley's first two books on human happiness are published together here—his rare collection of essays together with the novel which introduces his most famous character, the Masterful Monk.

$15.00 — 216 pages. Available at amazon.com.

CANDLELIGHT ATTIC & ODD JOB'S, by Cecily Hallack

Here are seven true stories in honour of the Seven Joys of Our Blessed Lady, and ten more invented ones about the delightful Barnabas Job, to make a comfortable book for those who are afraid of the dark.

$14.00 — 192 pages. Available at amazon.com.

THE HAPPINESS OF FATHER HAPPÉ, by Cecily Hallack

Shingle Bay did not know what to make of Fr. Savinius Happé. He was a cheerful, rotund Franciscan, a famous author of books on everything from Etruscan civilization to Alpine meadows to beetles, and someone who had never quite mastered the English language. His jovial demeanor concealed a wisdom that alternately bewildered, astonished, but ultimately won over the people of Shingle Bay.

$10.00 — 112 pages. Available at amazon.com.

THREE RELIGIOUS REBELS, by M. Raymond, O.C.S.O.

The stories of the three Saints who founded the Cistercian order—St. Robert of Molesme, St. Alberic, and St. Stephen Harding.

$17.00 — 294 pages. Available at amazon.com.

THE RED INN OF SAINT LYPHAR, by Anna T. Sadlier

Richard Duplessis is leaving his sweetheart to fight under Jambe d'Argent, when his envious rival denounces him to the Revolution. Can even his wily commander save him and his friends from the guillotine?

$13.00 — 168 pages. Available at amazon.com.

CON OF MISTY MOUNTAIN, by Mary T. Waggaman

"It had been a long night for Con. Just what had happened to him he was at first too dazed to know. Dennis had flung him into the smoking-room with no very gentle hand, turned the key and left him to himself. And, sinking down dully upon a rug that felt very soft and warm after the hard flight over the mountain, Con was glad to rest his bruised, aching limbs, his dizzy head, without any thought of what was to come upon him next."

$14.00 — 190 pages. Available at amazon.com.

NON-FICTION

THE STORY OF THE WAR IN LA VENDÉE AND THE LITTLE CHOUAN-NERIE, by George J. Hill, M.A.

The story of the brave French Catholics who rose up in arms against the revolutionary government.

$18.00 — 342 pages. Available at amazon.com.

THE AMERICAN HERESY, by Christopher Hollis

The history of America told through the lives of Thomas Jefferson, John C. Calhoun, Abraham Lincoln, and Woodrow Wilson.

$18.00 — 358 pages. Available at amazon.com.

CATHOLICISM AND SCOTLAND, by Compton Mackenzie

The little known history of the Scots who sought to defend their country and their Faith from the onslaught of Protestantism.

$12.00 — 138 pages. Available at amazon.com.

DOMINICAN SAINTS, by the Novices of the Dominican House of Studies

The astonishing lives of fourteen saints of the Dominican Order.

$19.00 — 392 pages. Available at amazon.com.